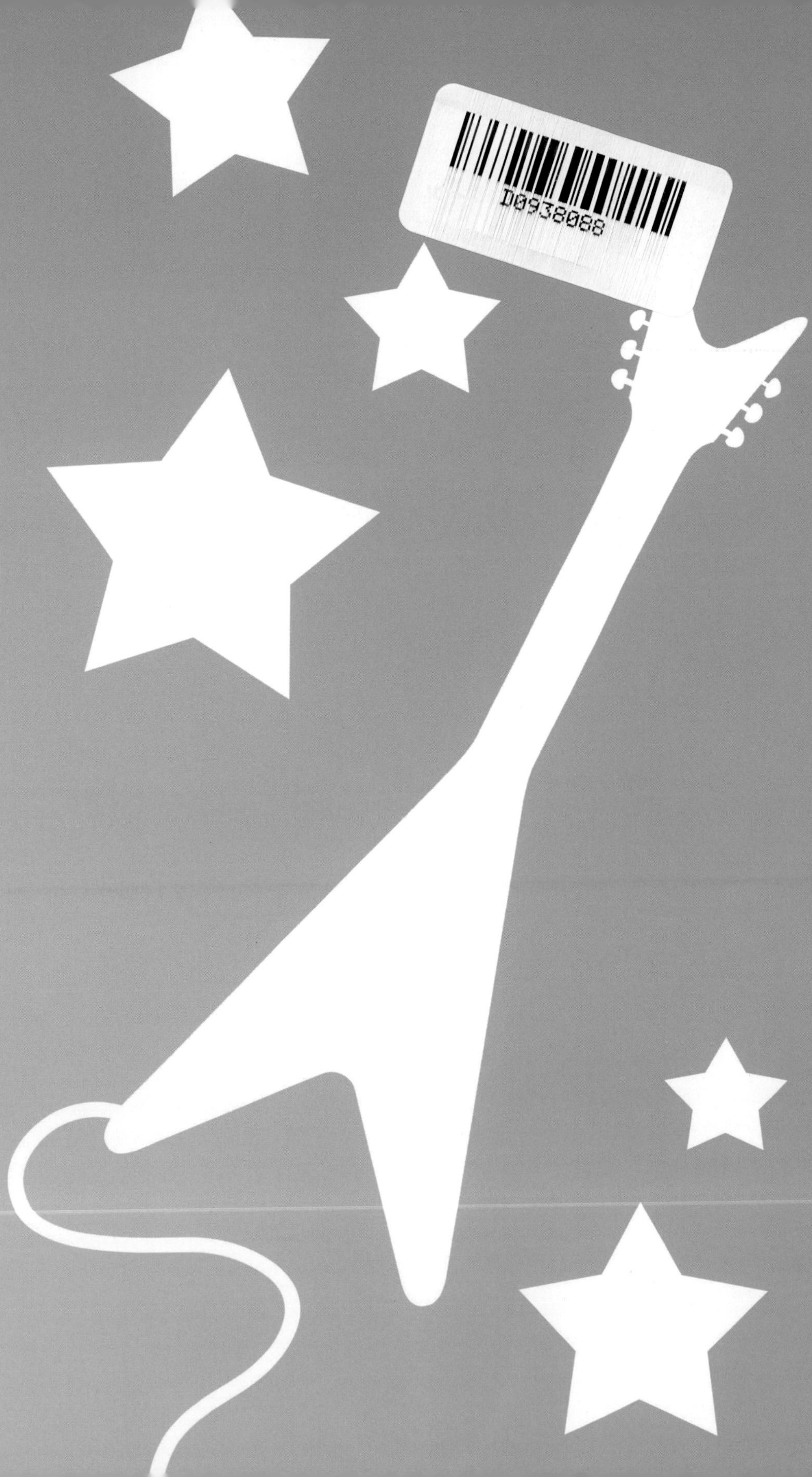

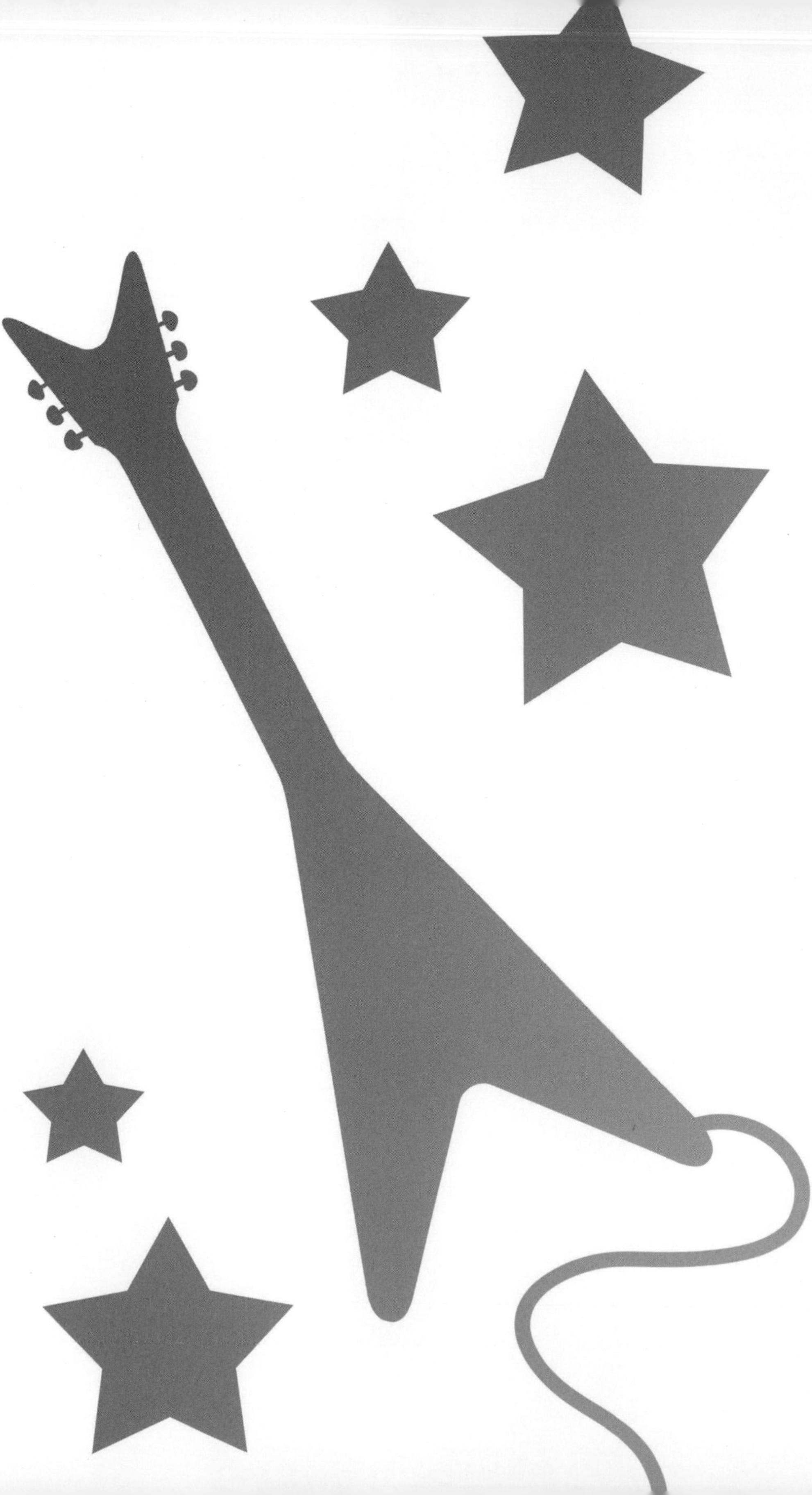

Pak · Coulton · Miyazawa
Kholinne · Farrell · Bowland

The PRINCESS who saved her FRIENDS ™

Published by
kaboom!

KaBOOM! Designer
Marie Krupina

KaBOOM! Edition Editor
Sophie Philips-Roberts

KaBOOM! Edition Assistant Editor
Kenzie Rzonca

KaBOOM! Edition Senior Editor
Shannon Watters

Ross Richie..Chairman & Founder
Matt Gagnon... Editor-in-Chief
Filip Sablik..................... President, Publishing & Marketing
Stephen Christy ....President, Development
Lance Kreiter ...... Vice President, Licensing & Merchandising
Bryce Carlson ....Vice President, Editorial & Creative Strategy
Kate Henning.................................Director, Operations
Elyse Strandberg.................................Manager, Finance
Michelle Ankley.....................Manager, Production Design
Sierra Hahn.................................... Executive Editor
Dafna Pleban ....Senior Editor
Shannon Watters ....Senior Editor
Eric Harburn ....Senior Editor
Elizabeth Brei ....Editor
Kathleen Wisneski ....Editor
Sophie Philips-Roberts.................................Editor
Jonathan Manning ....Associate Editor
Allyson Gronowitz ....Associate Editor
Gavin Gronenthal..................................Assistant Editor
Gwen Waller......................................Assistant Editor
Ramiro Portnoy....................................Assistant Editor
Kenzie Rzonca.....................................Assistant Editor

Rey Netschke ....Editorial Assistant
Marie Krupina.................................... Design Lead
Grace Park..................................Design Coordinator
Chelsea Roberts.....................................Design Coordinator
Madison Goyette ....Production Designer
Crystal White ....Production Designer
Samantha Knapp.....................Production Design Assistant
Esther Kim .... Marketing Lead
Breanna Sarpy.................................Marketing Lead, Digital
Amanda Lawson .... Marketing Coordinator
Grecia Martinez ....Marketing Assistant, Digital
José Meza.....................................Consumer Sales Lead
Ashley Troub .... Consumer Sales Coordinator
Morgan Perry ....Retail Sales Lead
Harley Salbacka .... Sales Coordinator
Megan Christopher .... Operations Coordinator
Rodrigo Hernandez .... Operations Coordinator
Zipporah Smith .... Operations Coordinator
Jason Lee .... Senior Accountant
Sabrina Lesin .... Accounting Assistant
Lauren Alexander ....Administrative Assistant

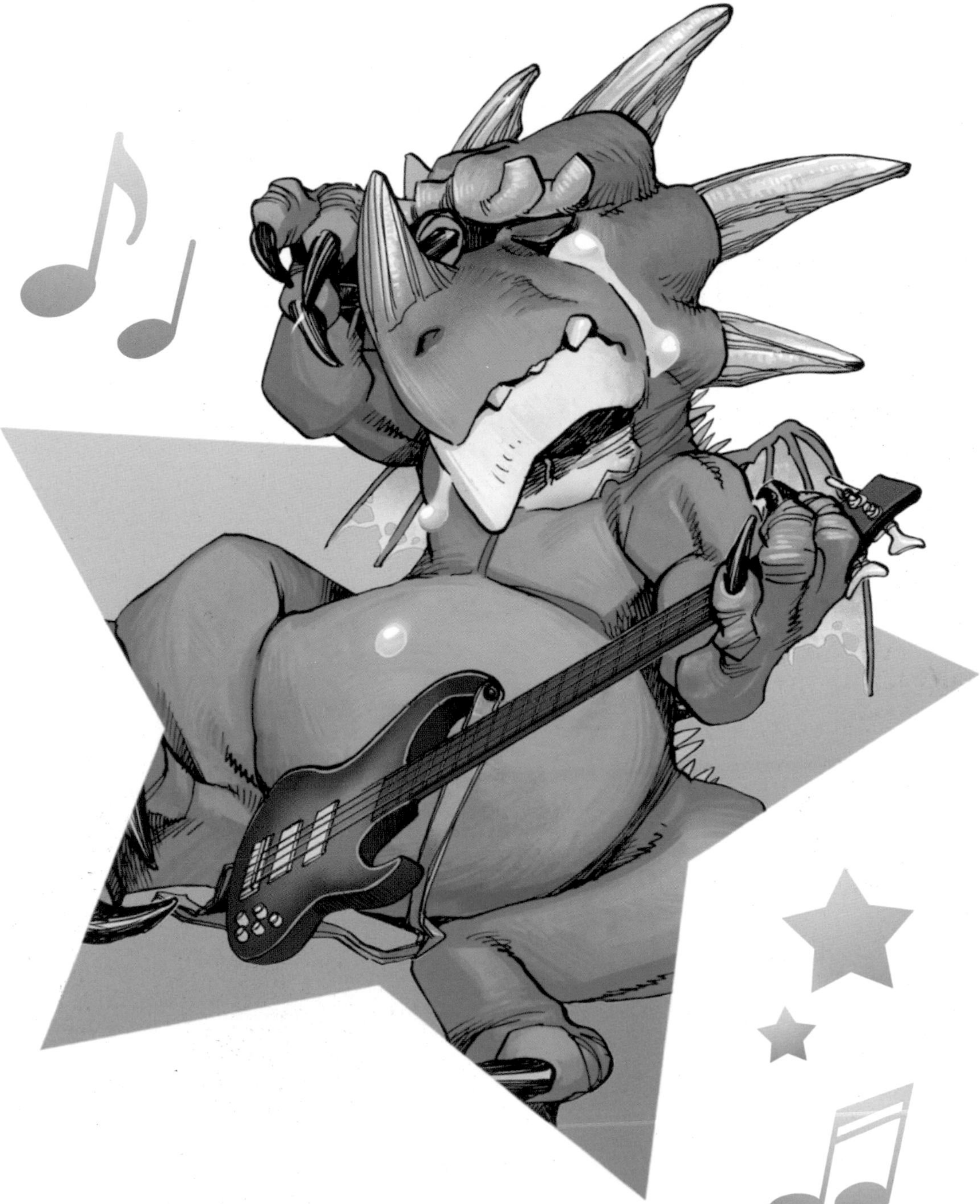

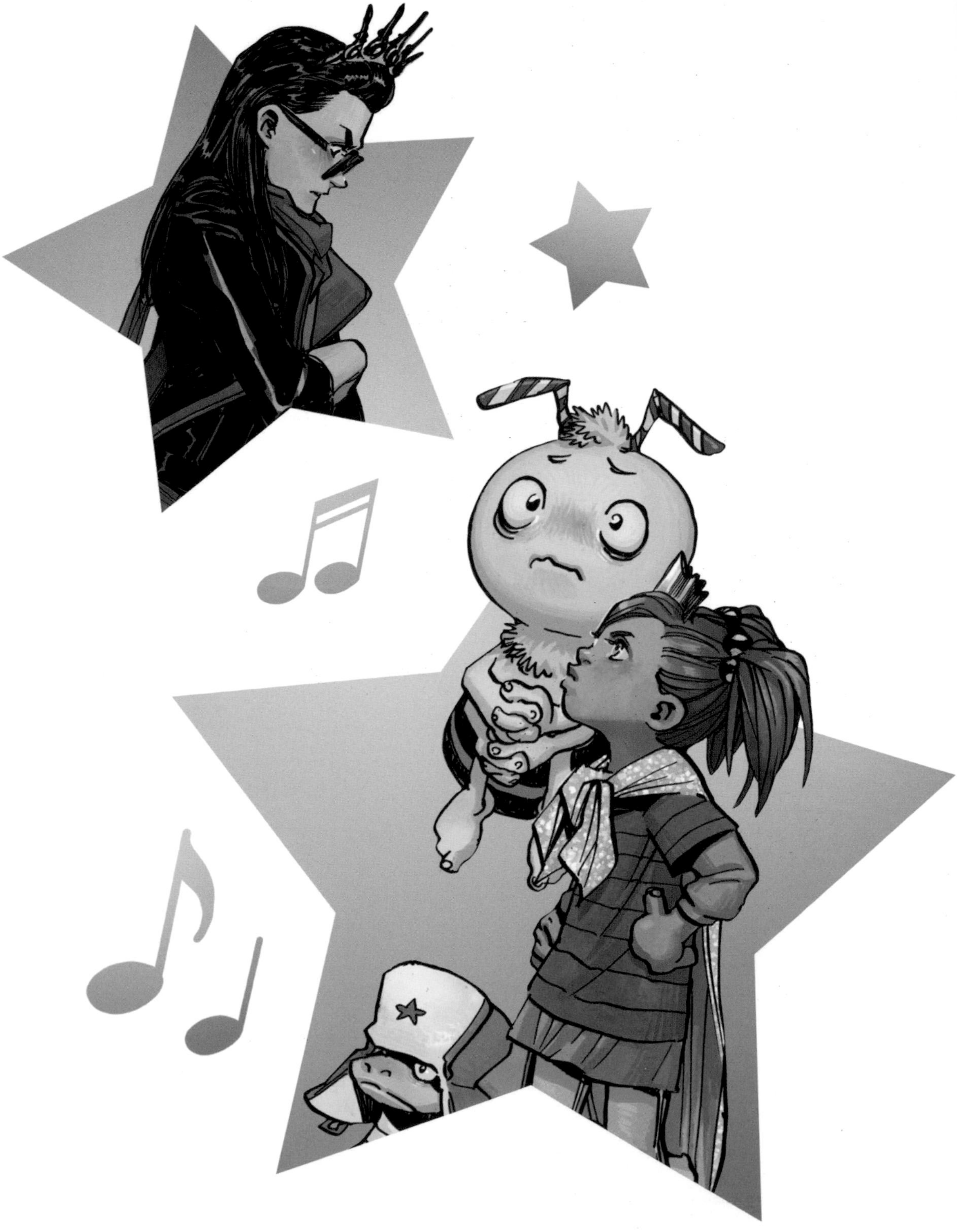

The PRINCESS who saved her FRIENDS™

Written by
GREG PAK and **JONATHAN COULTON**

Based on the song by
JONATHAN COULTON

Art by
TAKESHI MIYAZAWA

Colors by
JESSICA KHOLINNE
and **TRIONA FARRELL**

Letters by
SIMON BOWLAND

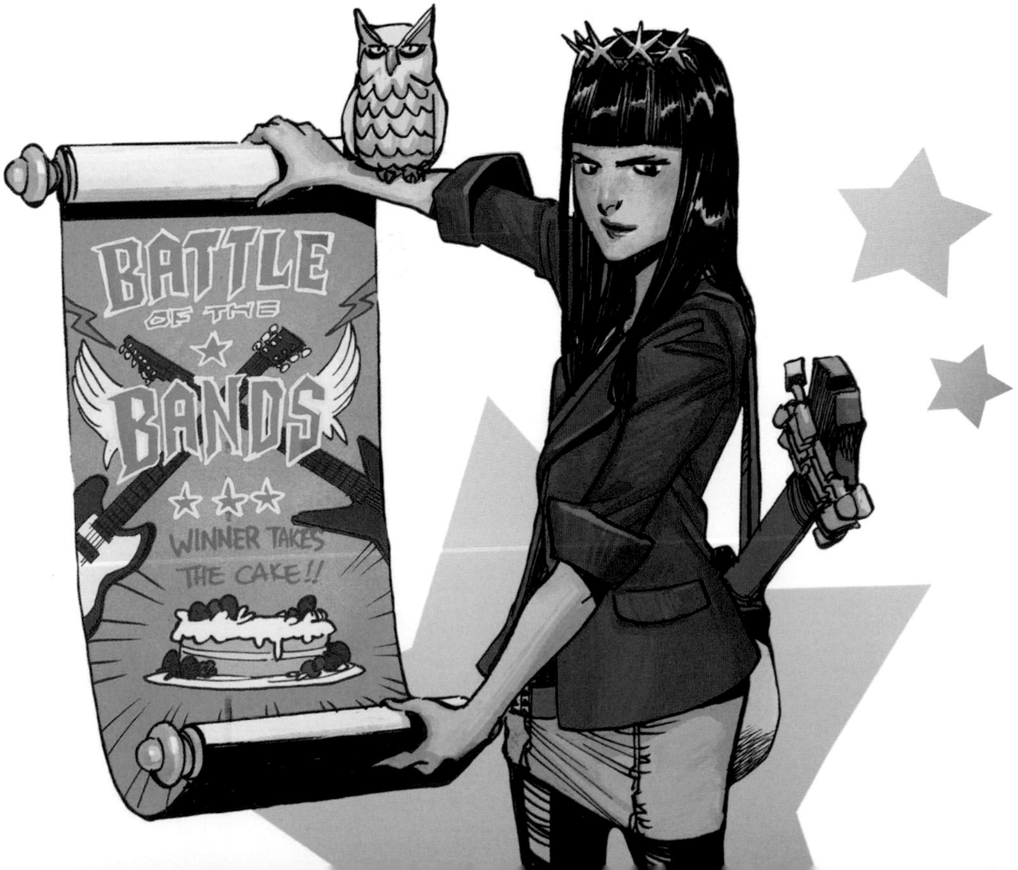

BATTLE
OF THE
BANDS
WINNER TAKES
THE CAKE!!

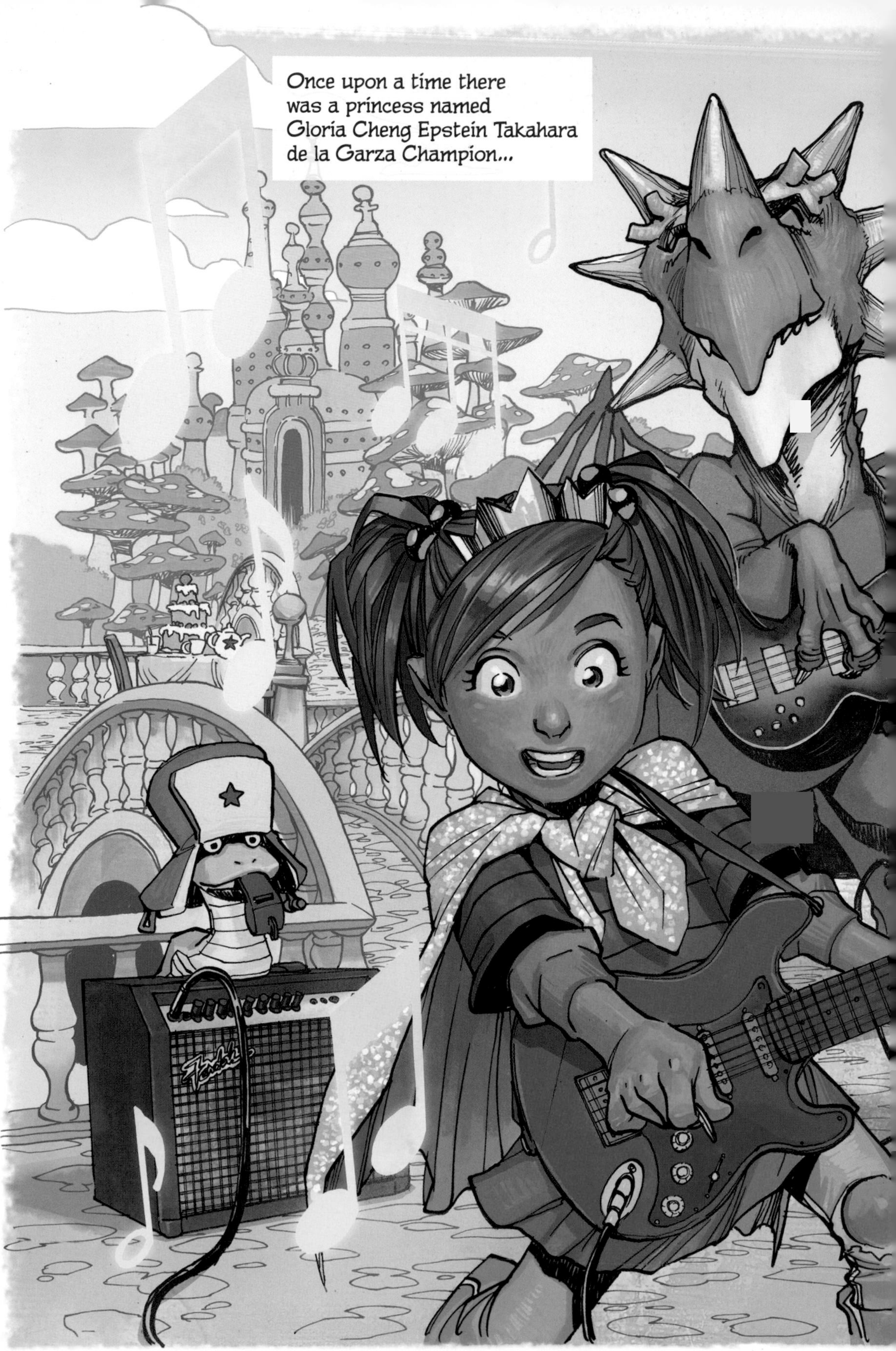
Once upon a time there was a princess named Gloria Cheng Epstein Takahara de la Garza Champion...

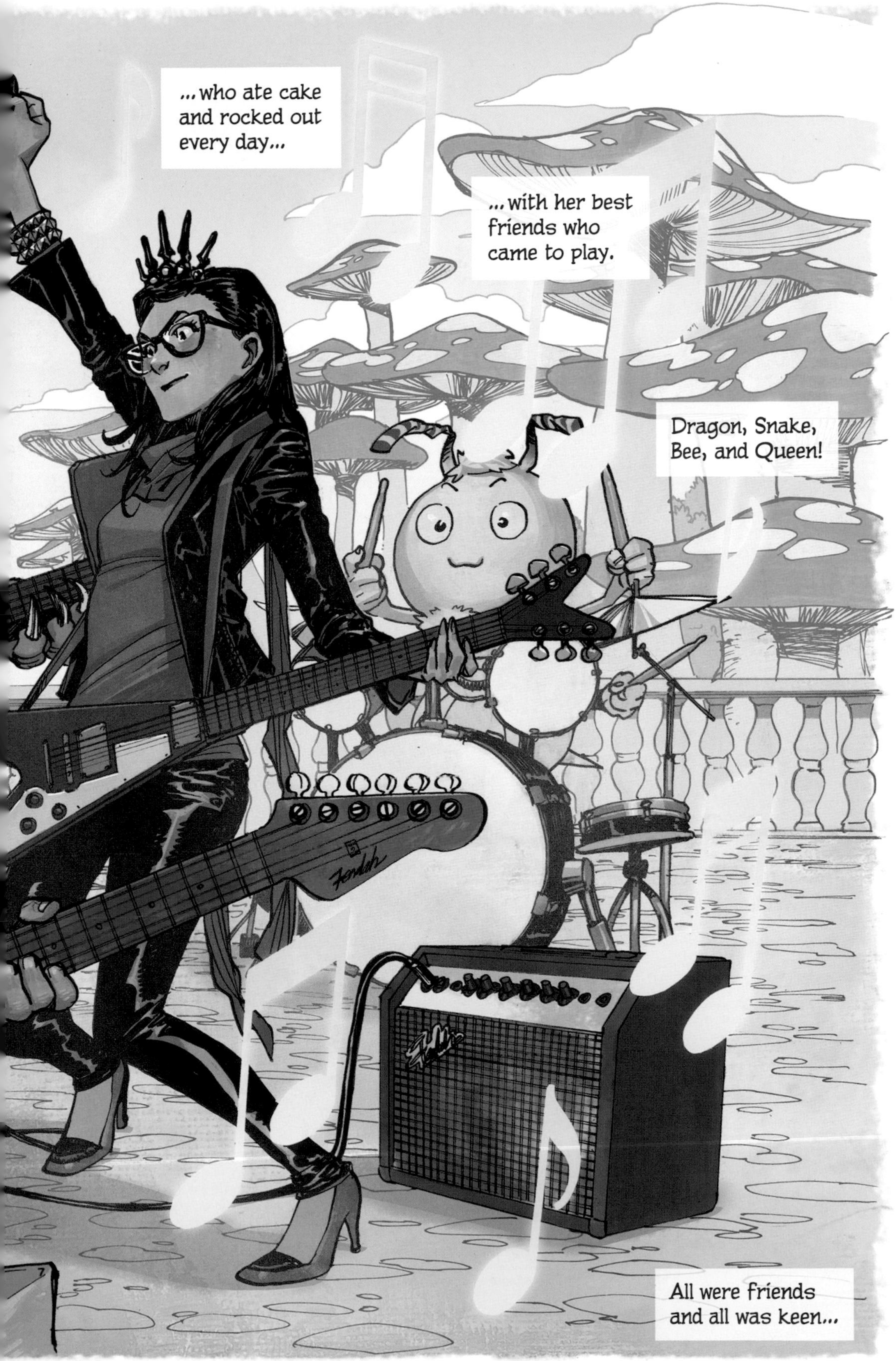
...who ate cake and rocked out every day...
...with her best friends who came to play.
Dragon, Snake, Bee, and Queen!
All were friends and all was keen...

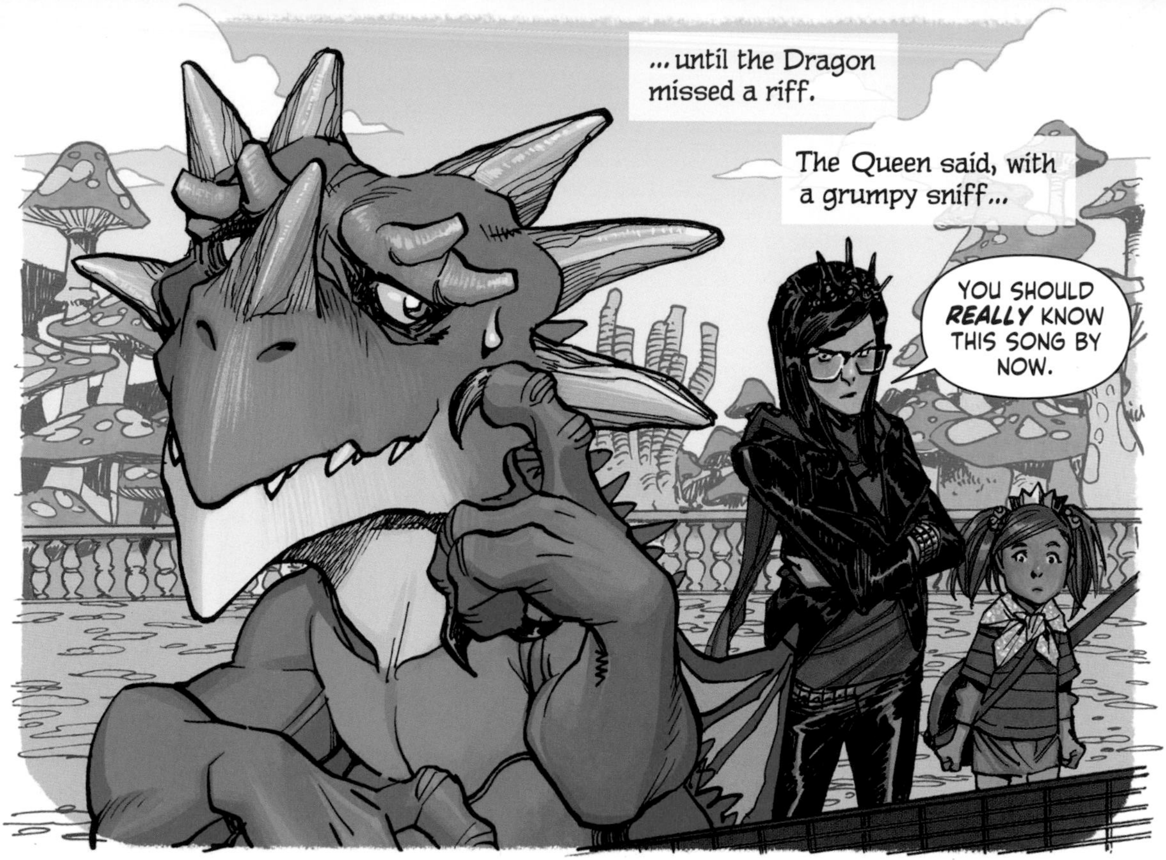
...until the Dragon missed a riff.
The Queen said, with a grumpy sniff...
YOU SHOULD **REALLY** KNOW THIS SONG BY NOW.

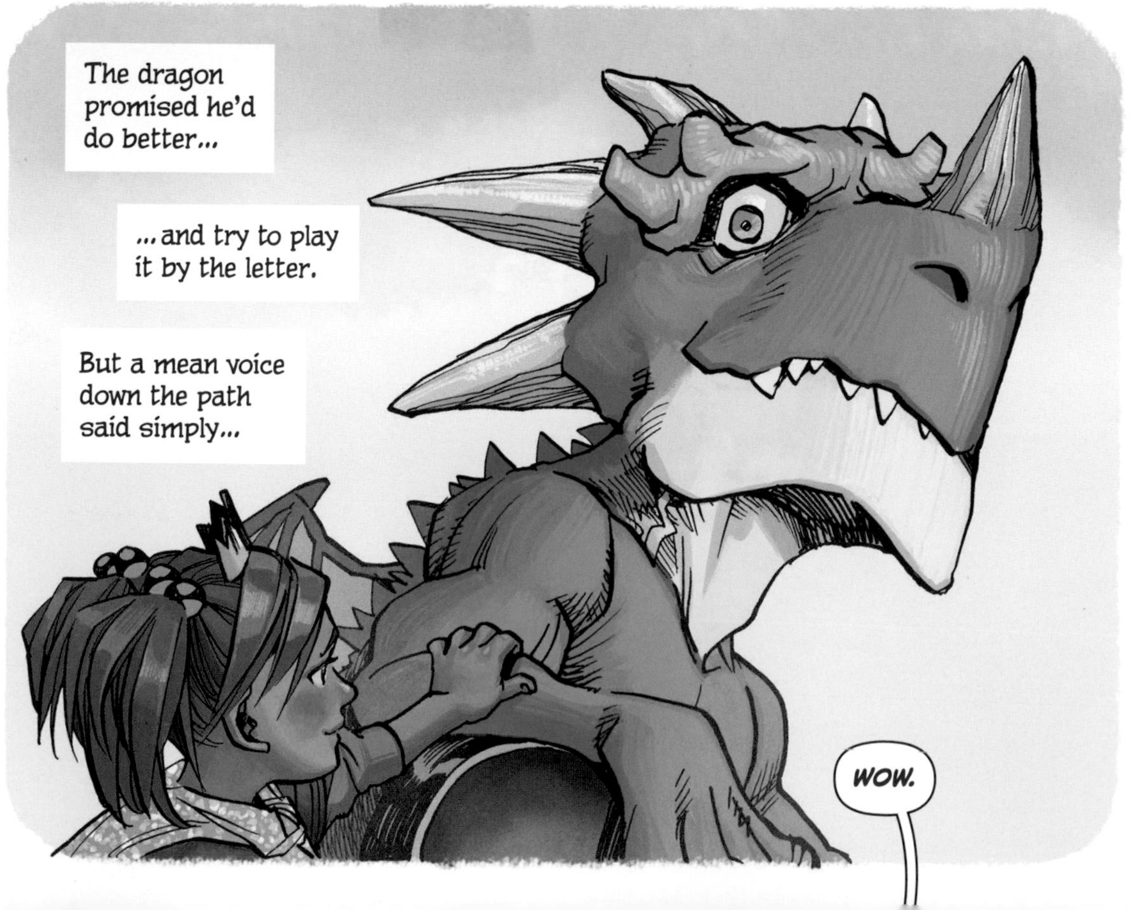
The dragon promised he'd do better...
...and try to play it by the letter.
But a mean voice down the path said simply...
WOW.

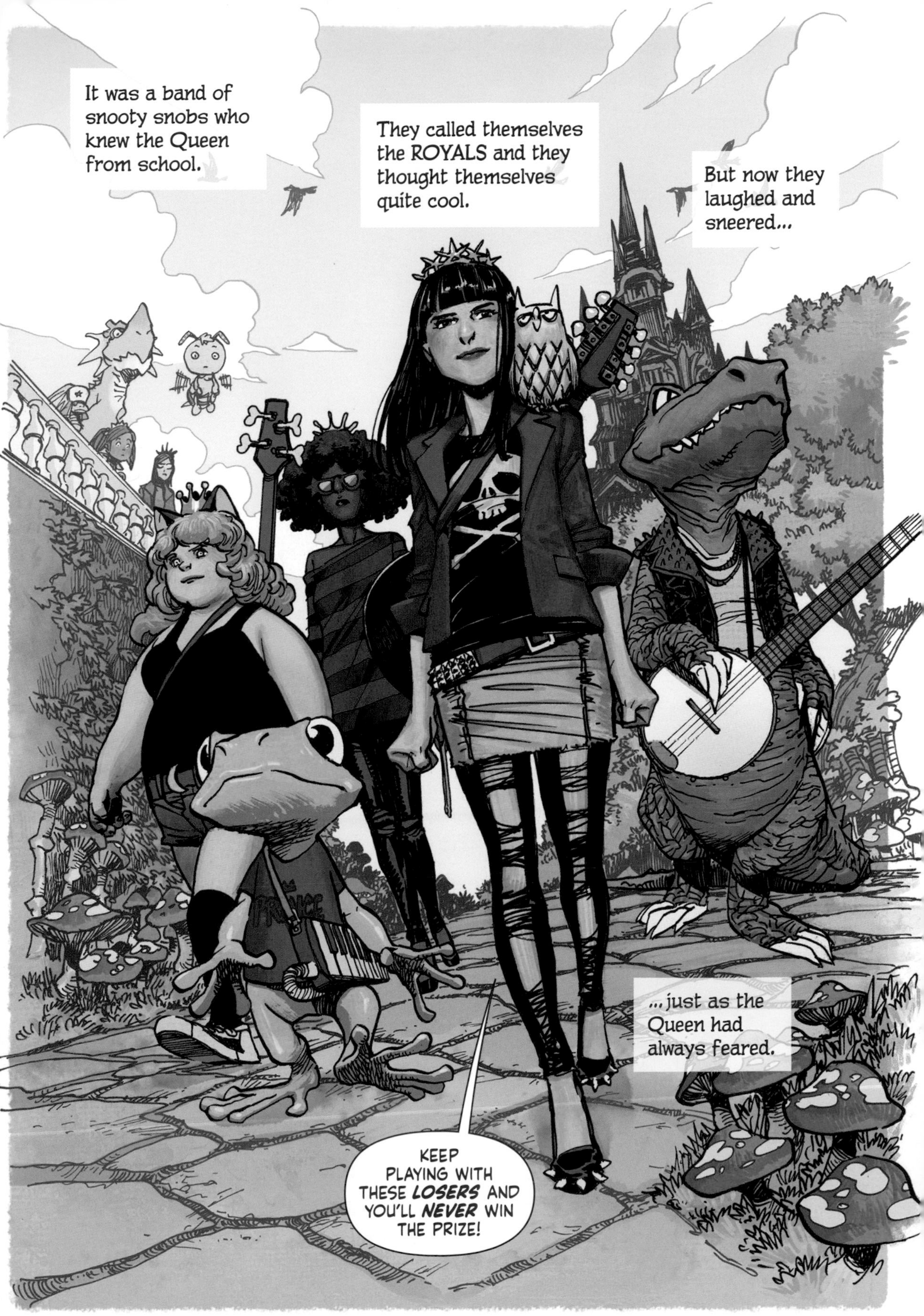
It was a band of snooty snobs who knew the Queen from school.
They called themselves the ROYALS and they thought themselves quite cool.
But now they laughed and sneered...
...just as the Queen had always feared.
KEEP PLAYING WITH THESE ***LOSERS*** AND YOU'LL ***NEVER*** WIN THE PRIZE!

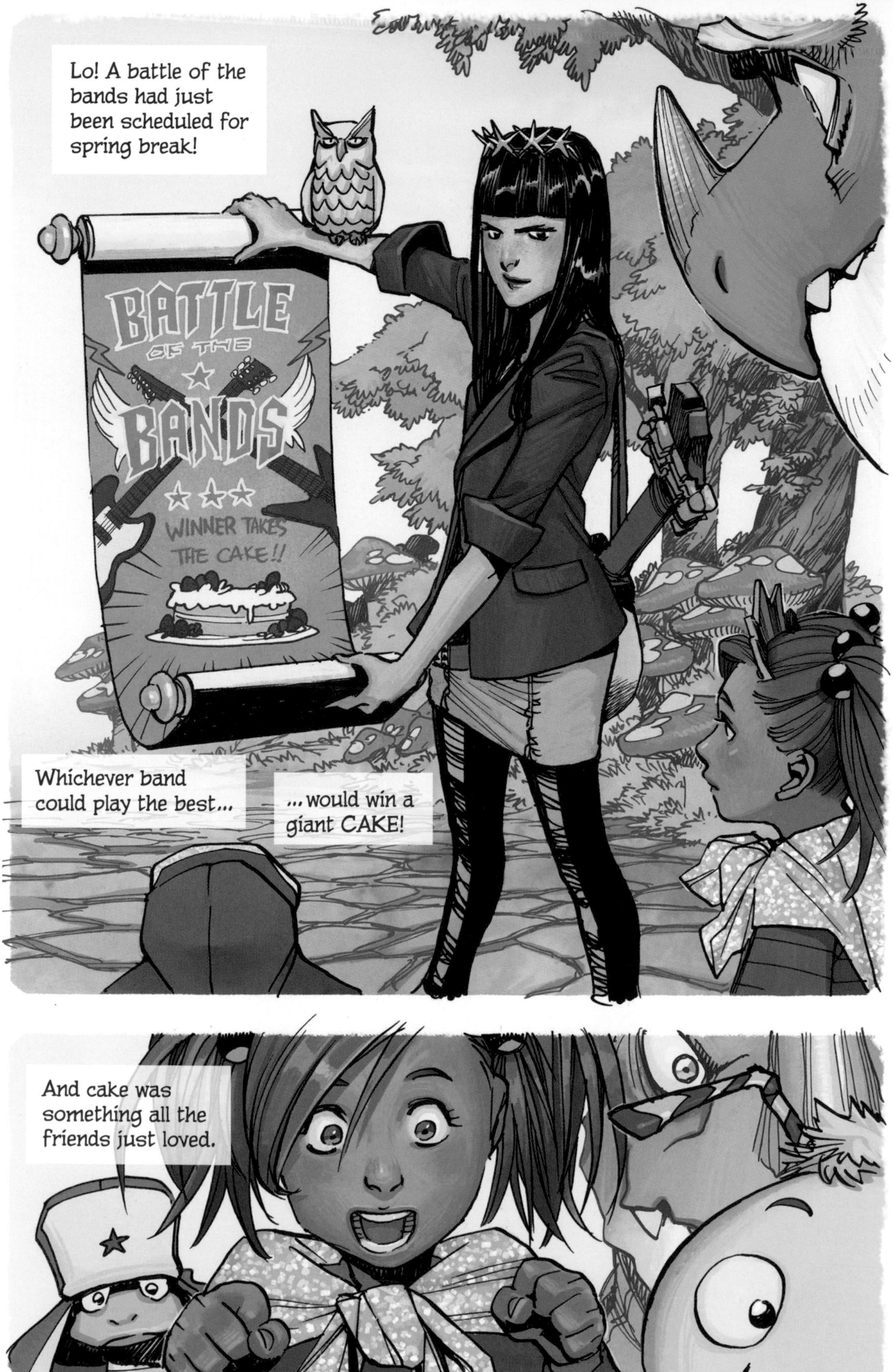
Lo! A battle of the bands had just been scheduled for spring break!
BATTLE OF THE BANDS
WINNER TAKES THE CAKE!!
Whichever band could play the best...
...would win a giant CAKE!
And cake was something all the friends just loved.

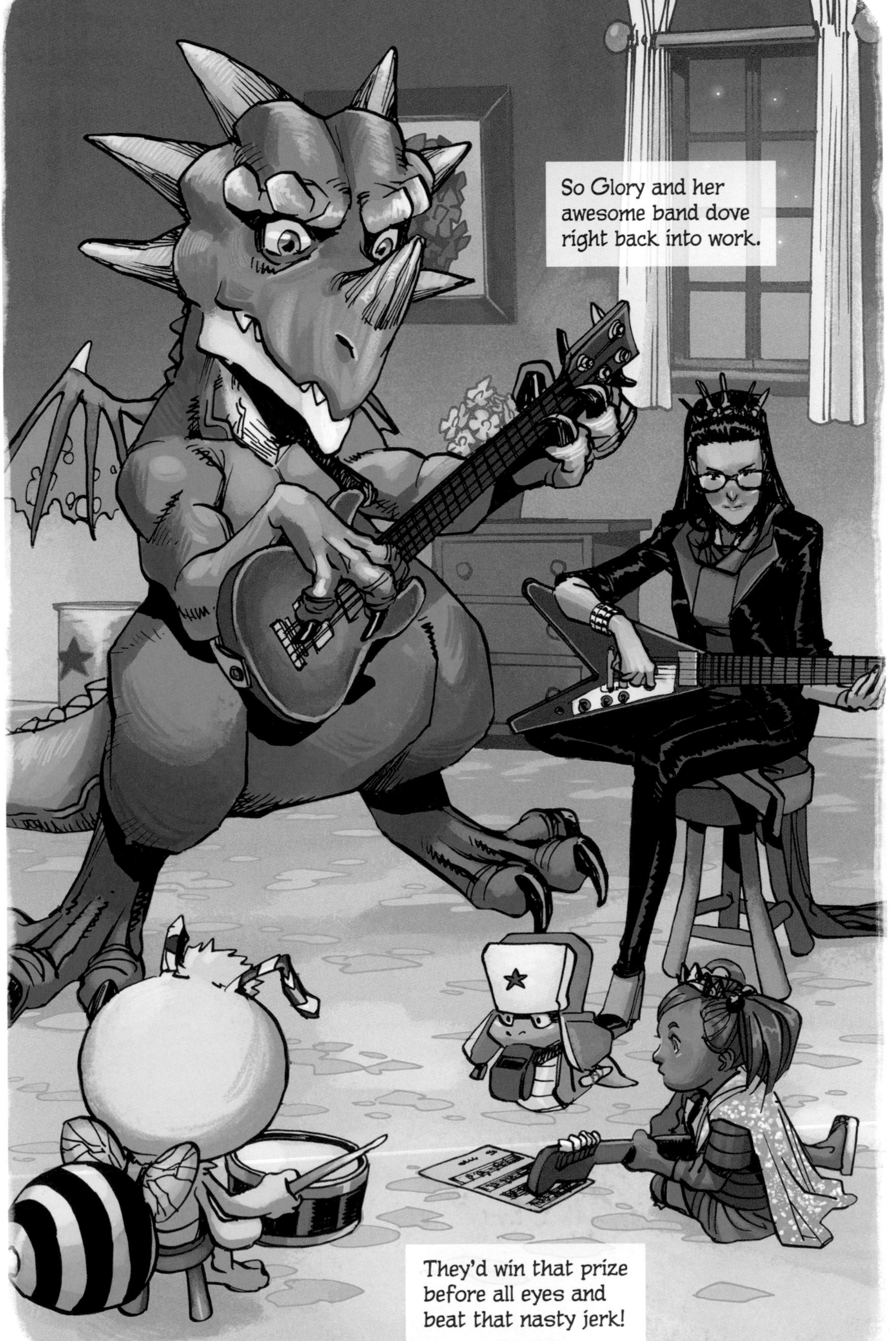
So Glory and her awesome band dove right back into work.
They'd win that prize before all eyes and beat that nasty jerk!

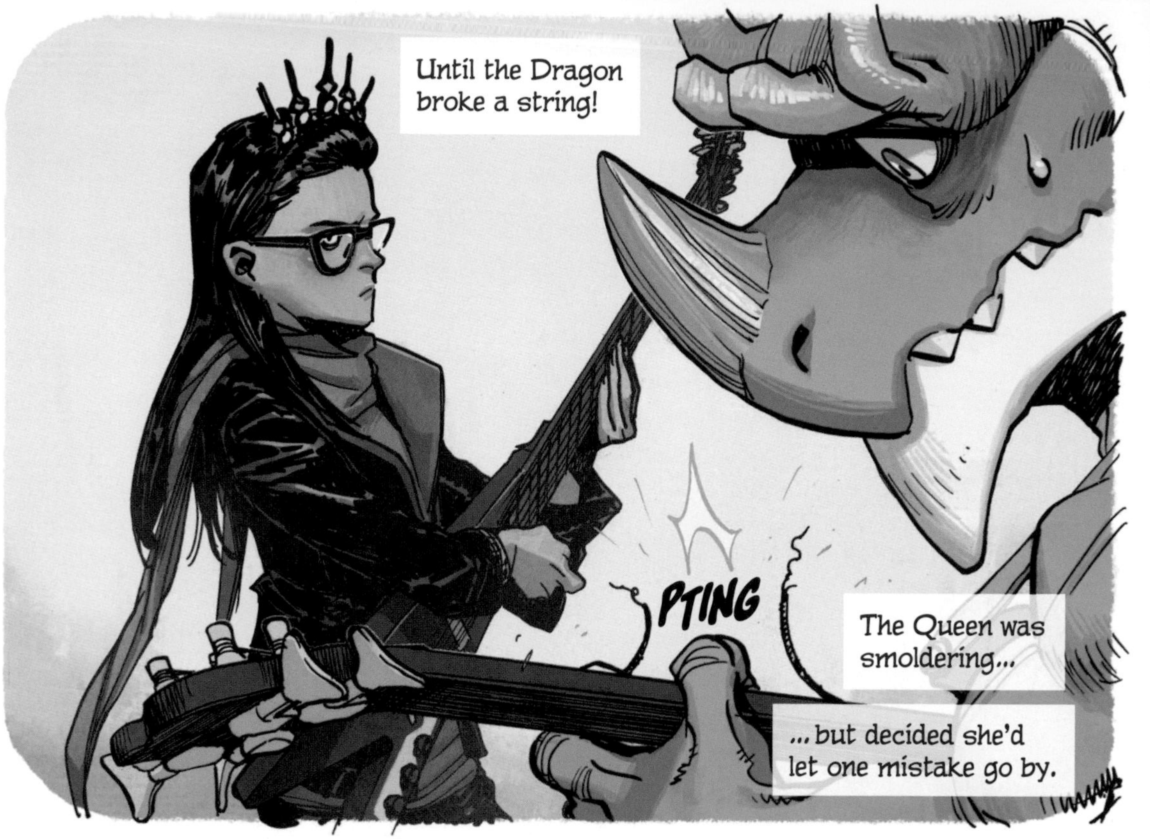
Until the Dragon broke a string!
PTING
The Queen was smoldering...
...but decided she'd let one mistake go by.

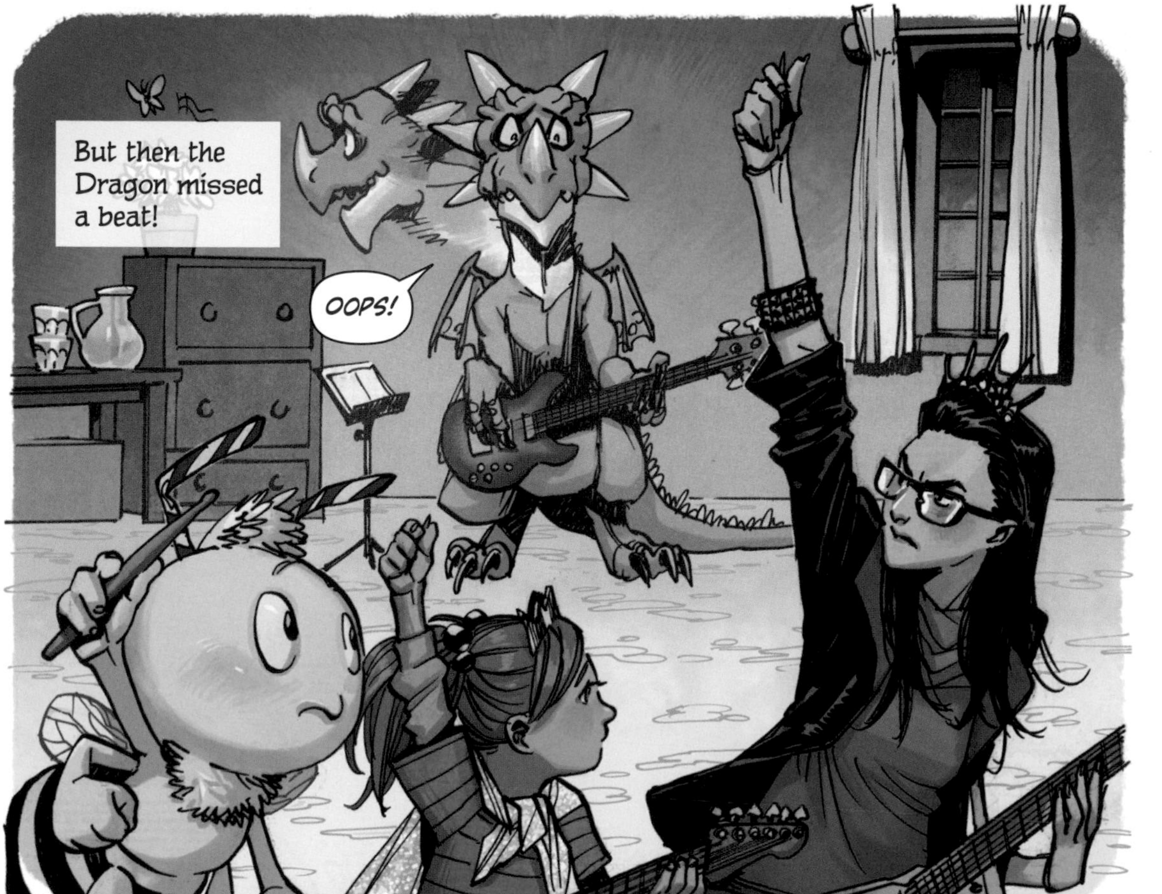
But then the Dragon missed a beat!
OOPS!

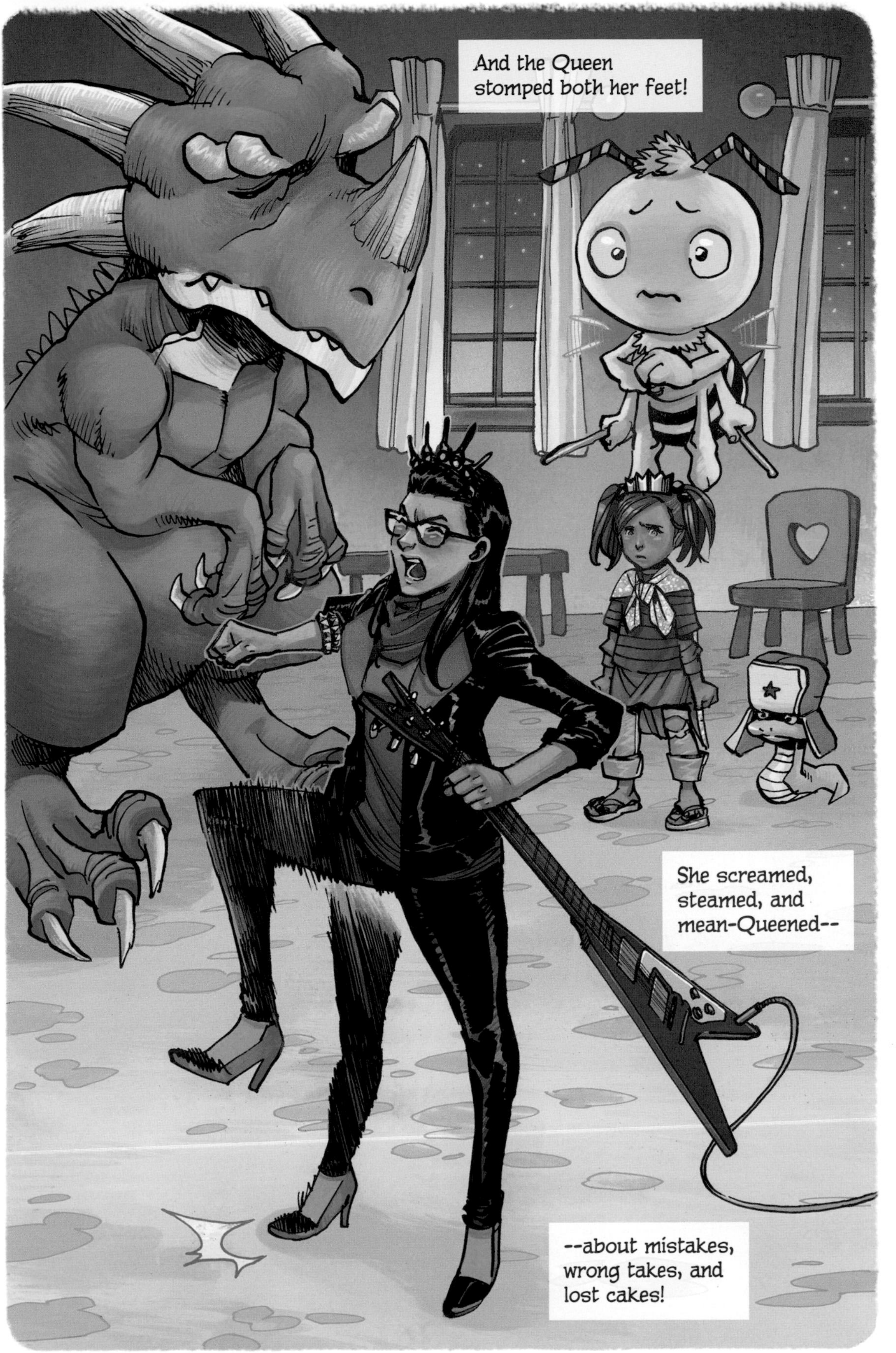
And the Queen stomped both her feet!
She screamed, steamed, and mean-Queened--
--about mistakes, wrong takes, and lost cakes!

And finally
she made the
Dragon cry.

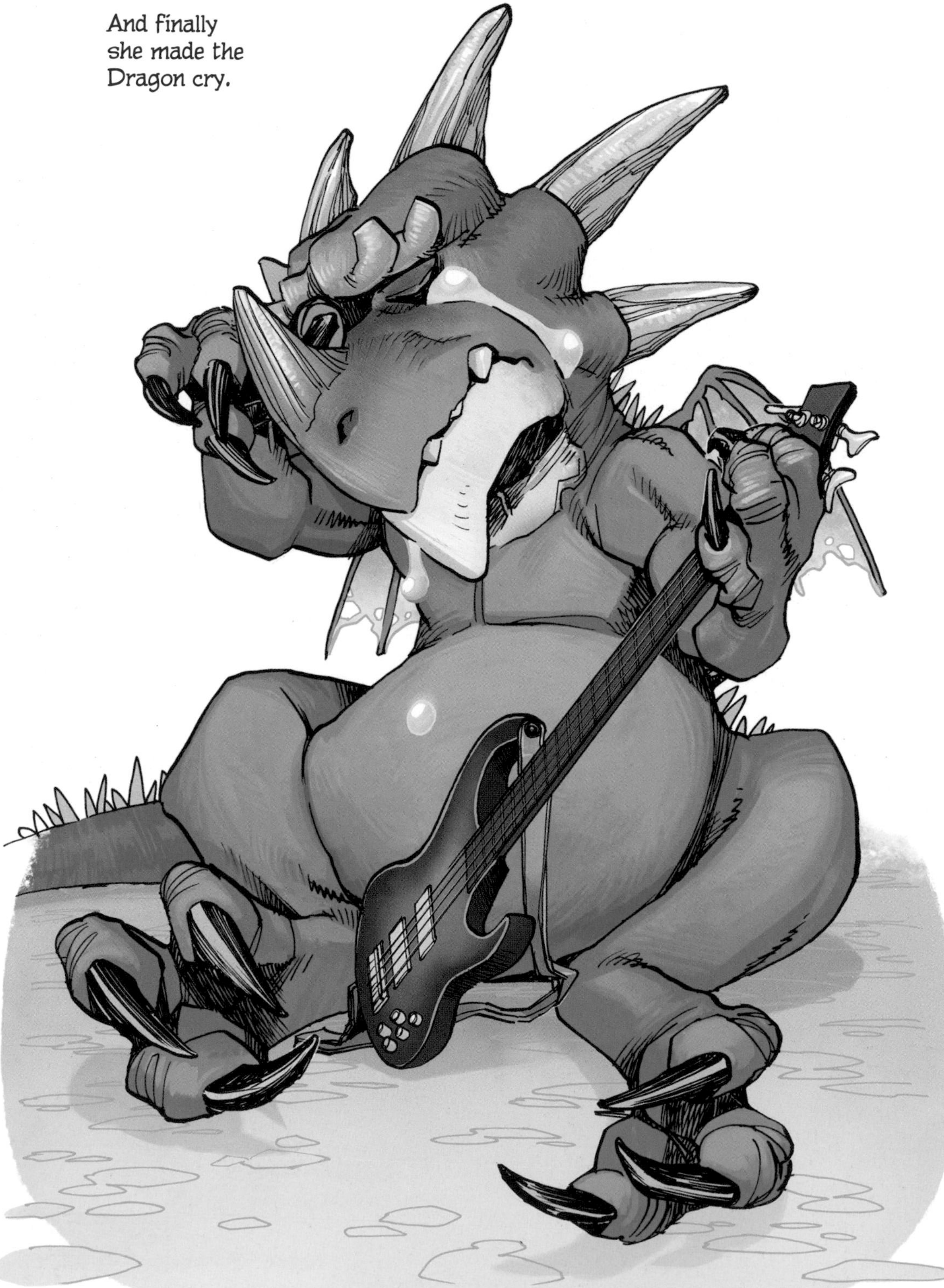

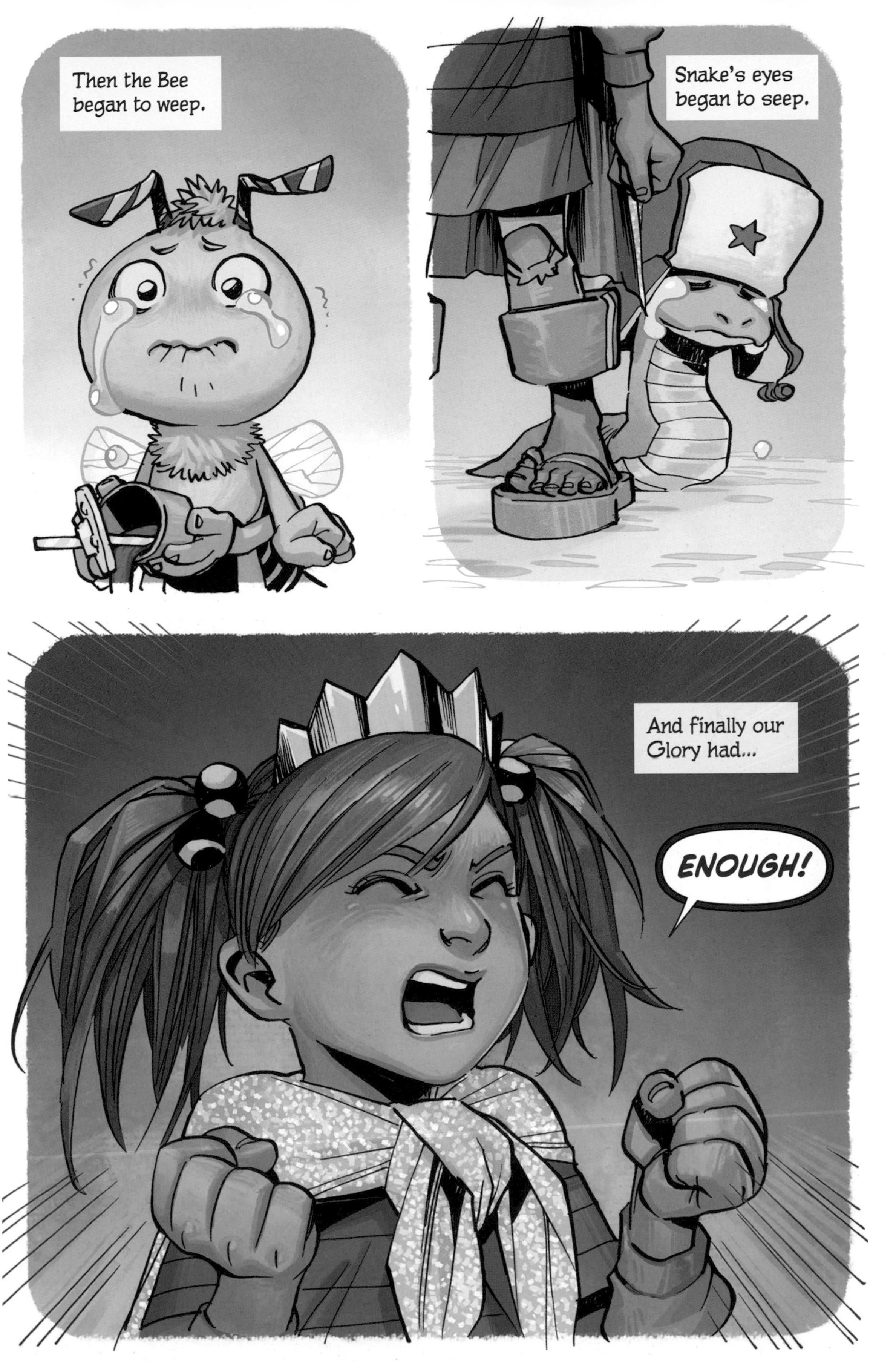
Then the Bee began to weep.
Snake's eyes began to seep.
And finally our Glory had...
ENOUGH!

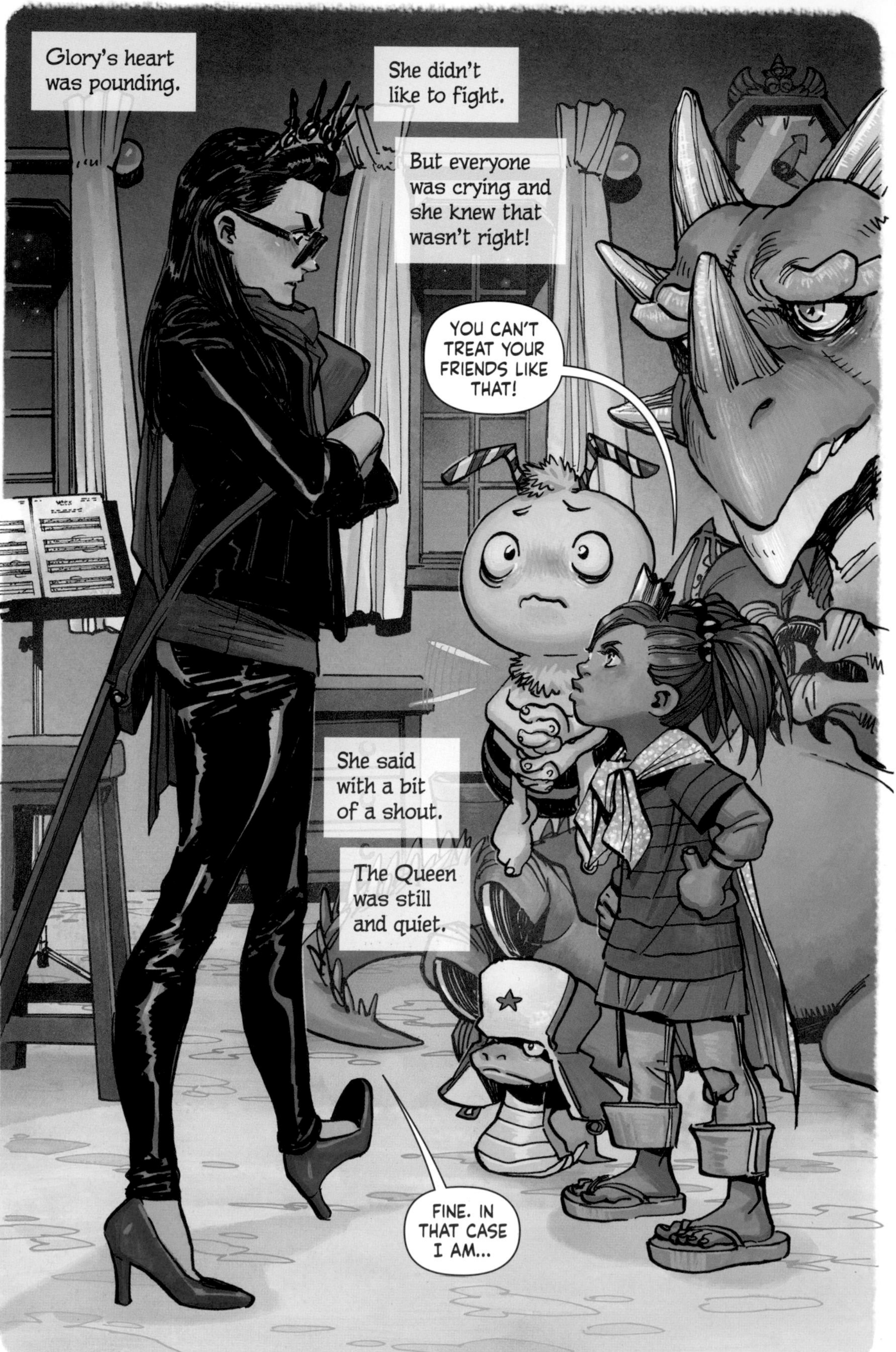

Glory's heart was pounding.
She didn't like to fight.
But everyone was crying and she knew that wasn't right!
YOU CAN'T TREAT YOUR FRIENDS LIKE THAT!
She said with a bit of a shout.
The Queen was still and quiet.
FINE. IN THAT CASE I AM...

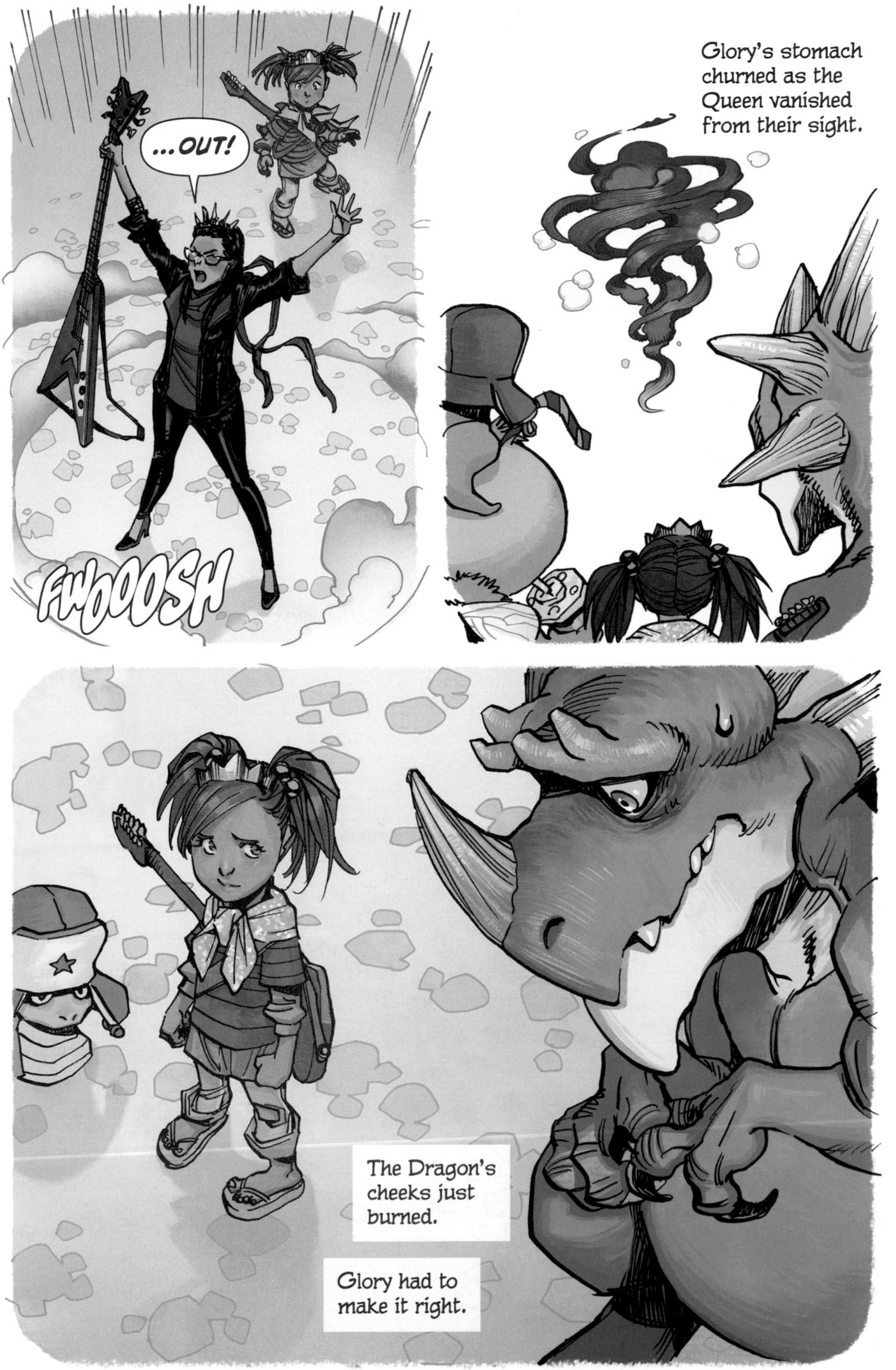
...OUT!
FWOOOSH
Glory's stomach churned as the Queen vanished from their sight.
The Dragon's cheeks just burned.
Glory had to make it right.

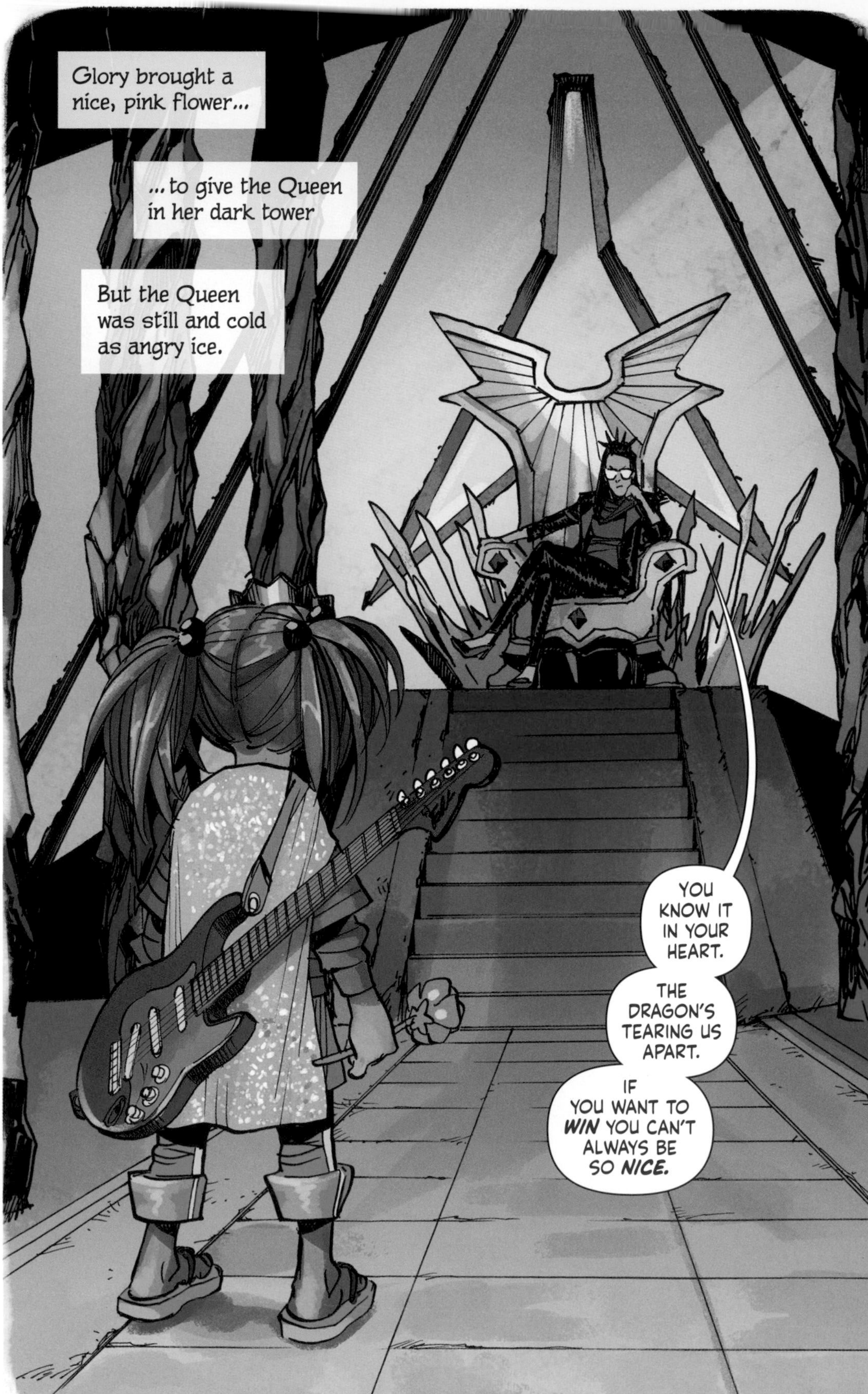

Glory brought a nice, pink flower...
...to give the Queen in her dark tower
But the Queen was still and cold as angry ice.
YOU KNOW IT IN YOUR HEART.
THE DRAGON'S TEARING US APART.
IF YOU WANT TO WIN YOU CAN'T ALWAYS BE SO NICE.

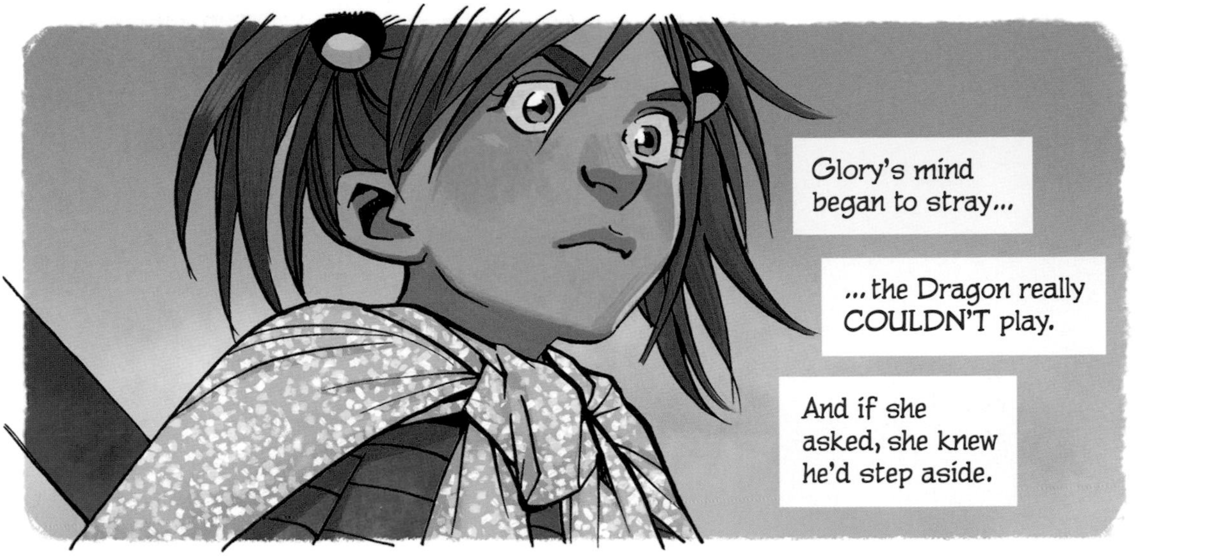
Glory's mind began to stray...
...the Dragon really COULDN'T play.
And if she asked, she knew he'd step aside.

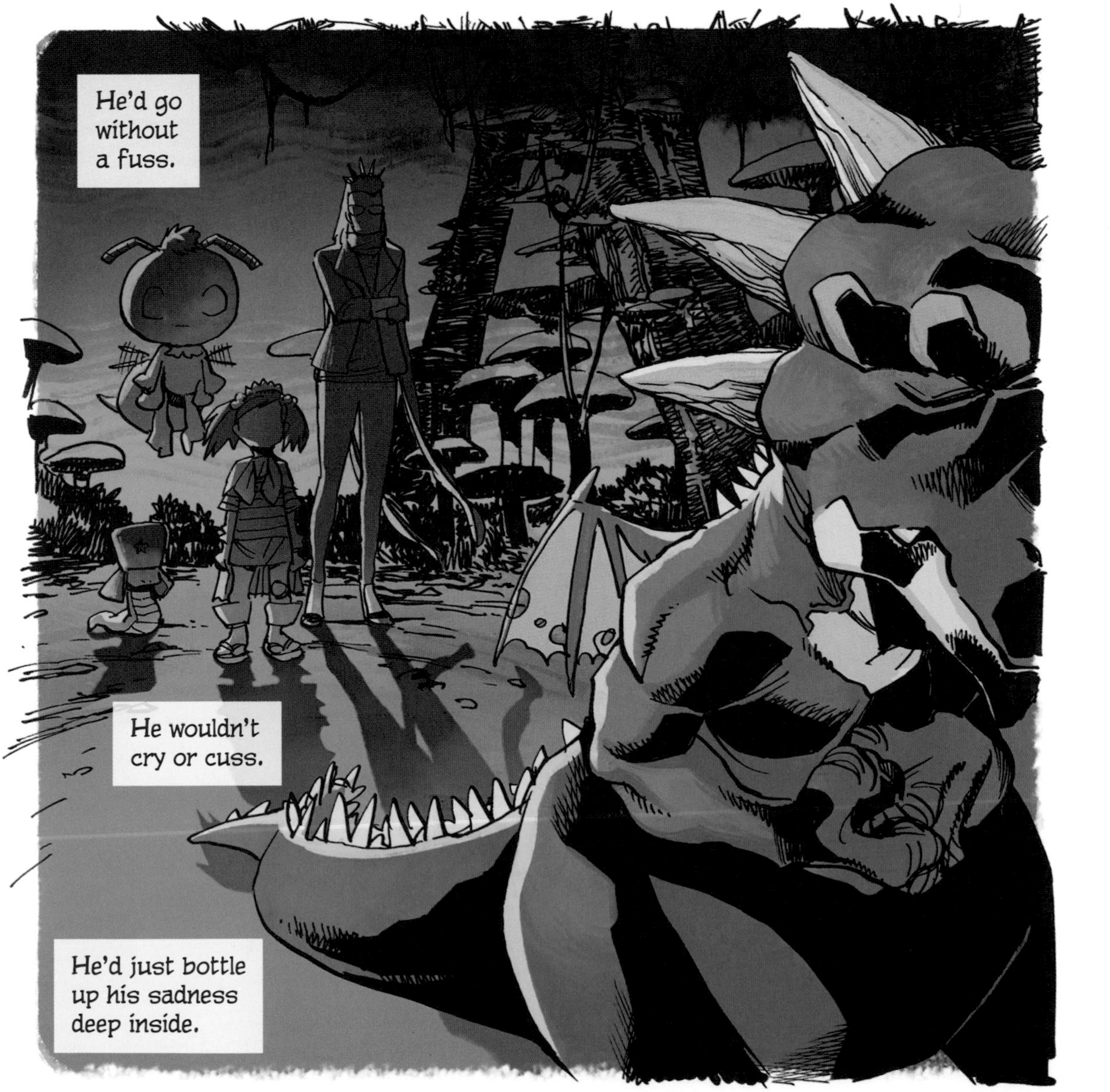
He'd go without a fuss.
He wouldn't cry or cuss.
He'd just bottle up his sadness deep inside.

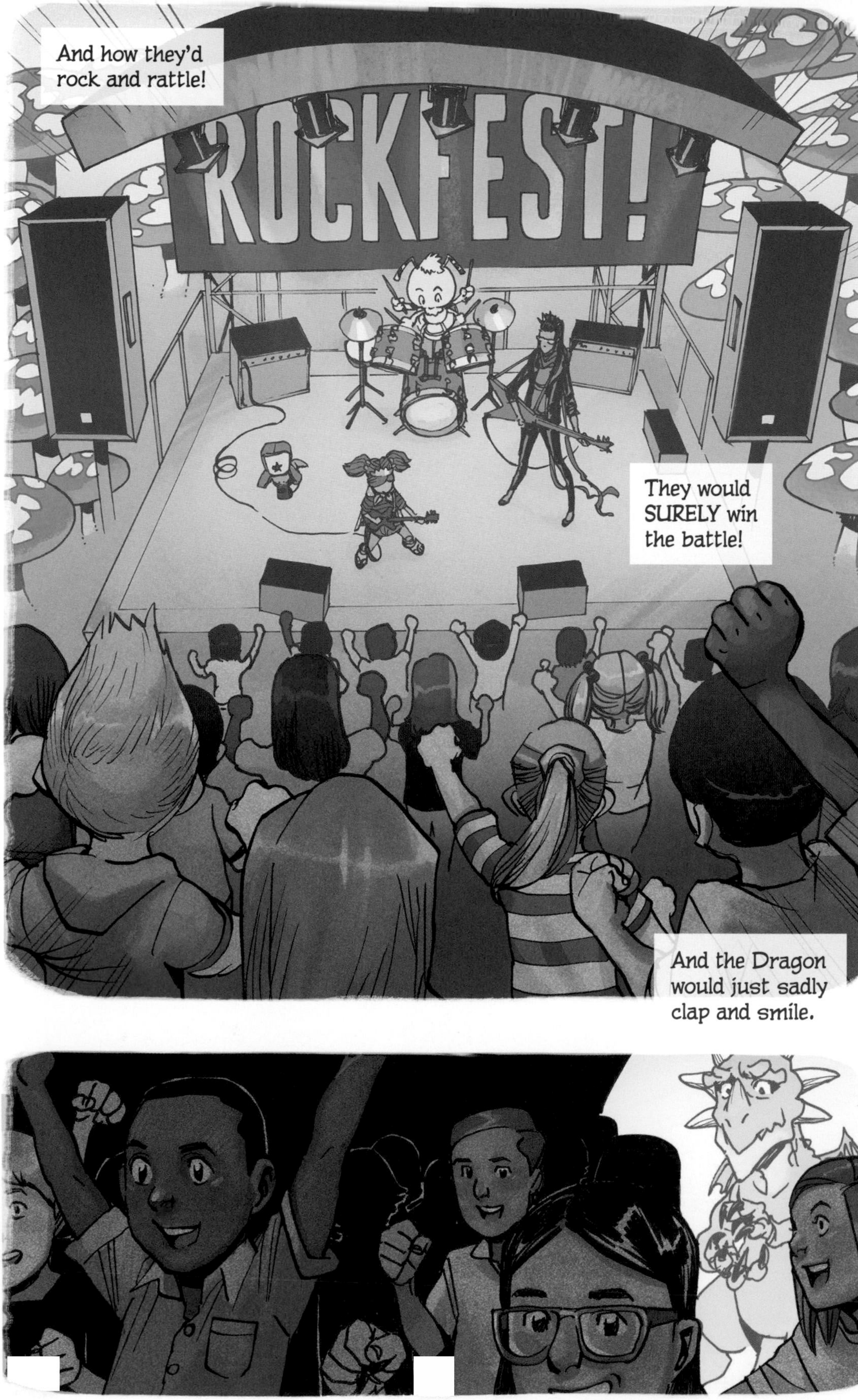

And how they'd rock and rattle!
ROCKFEST!
They would SURELY win the battle!
And the Dragon would just sadly clap and smile.

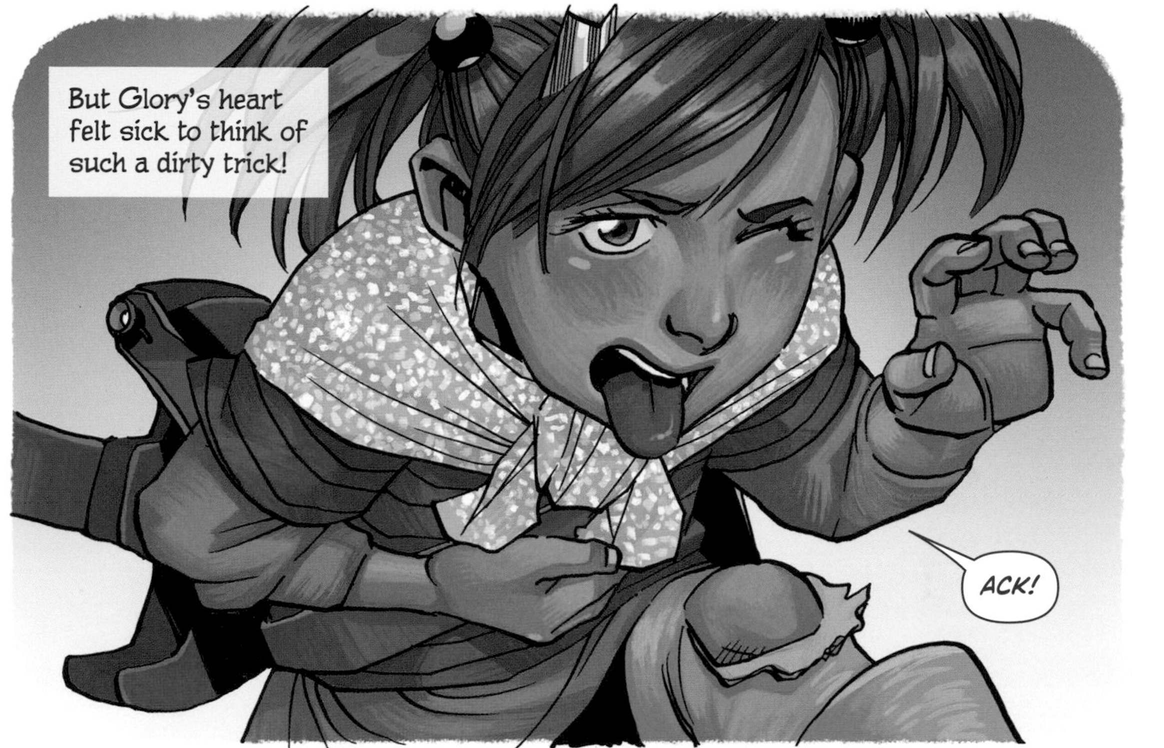
But Glory's heart felt sick to think of such a dirty trick!
ACK!

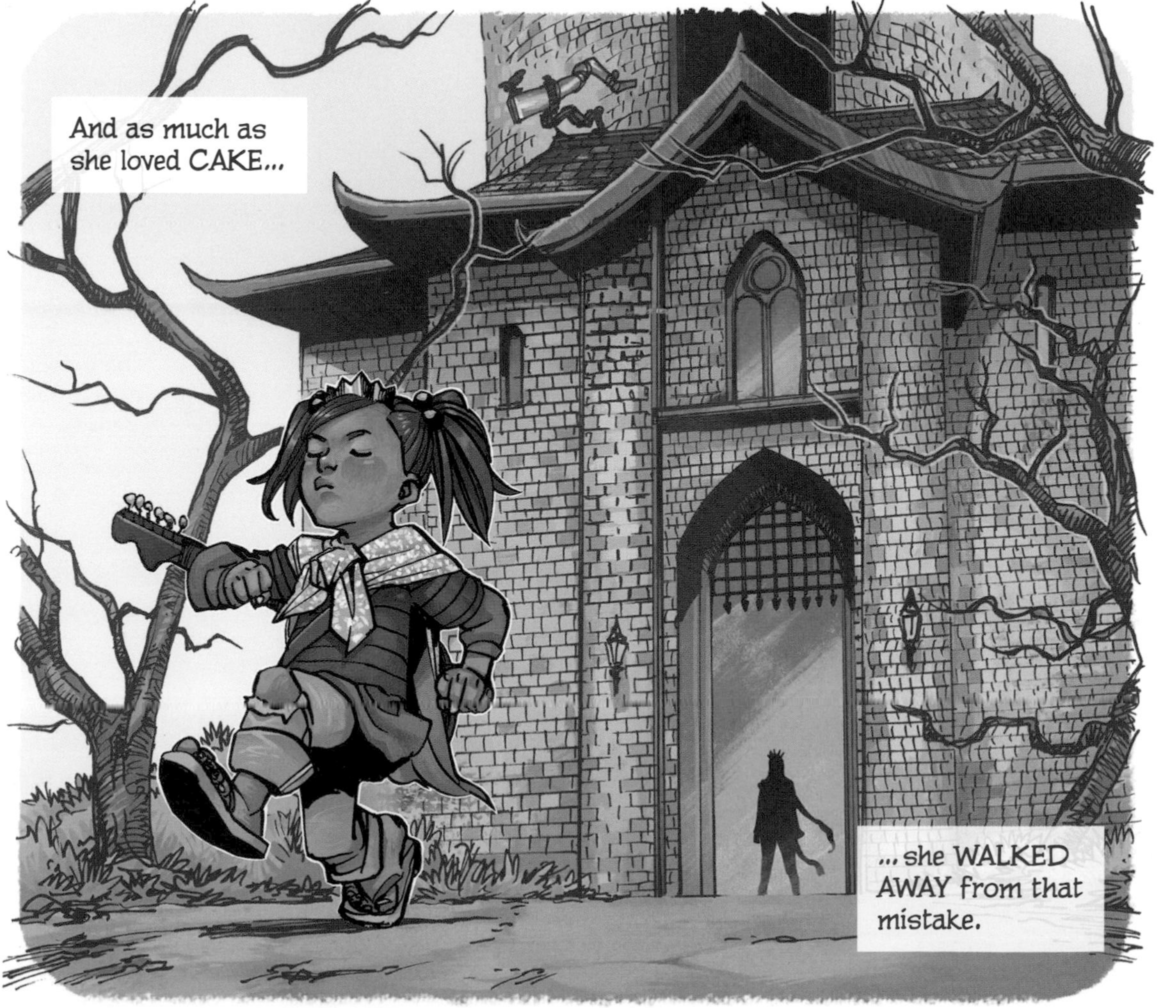
And as much as she loved CAKE...
... she WALKED AWAY from that mistake.

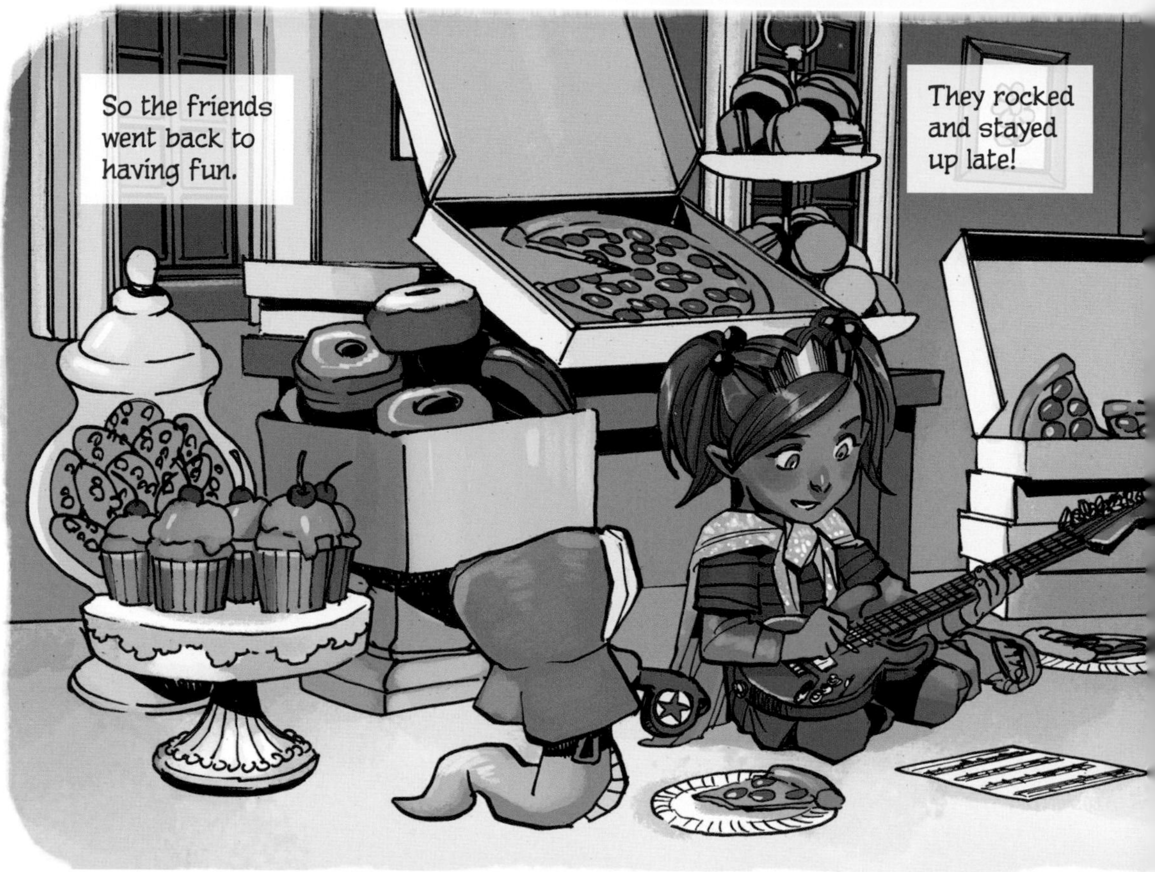
So the friends went back to having fun.
They rocked and stayed up late!

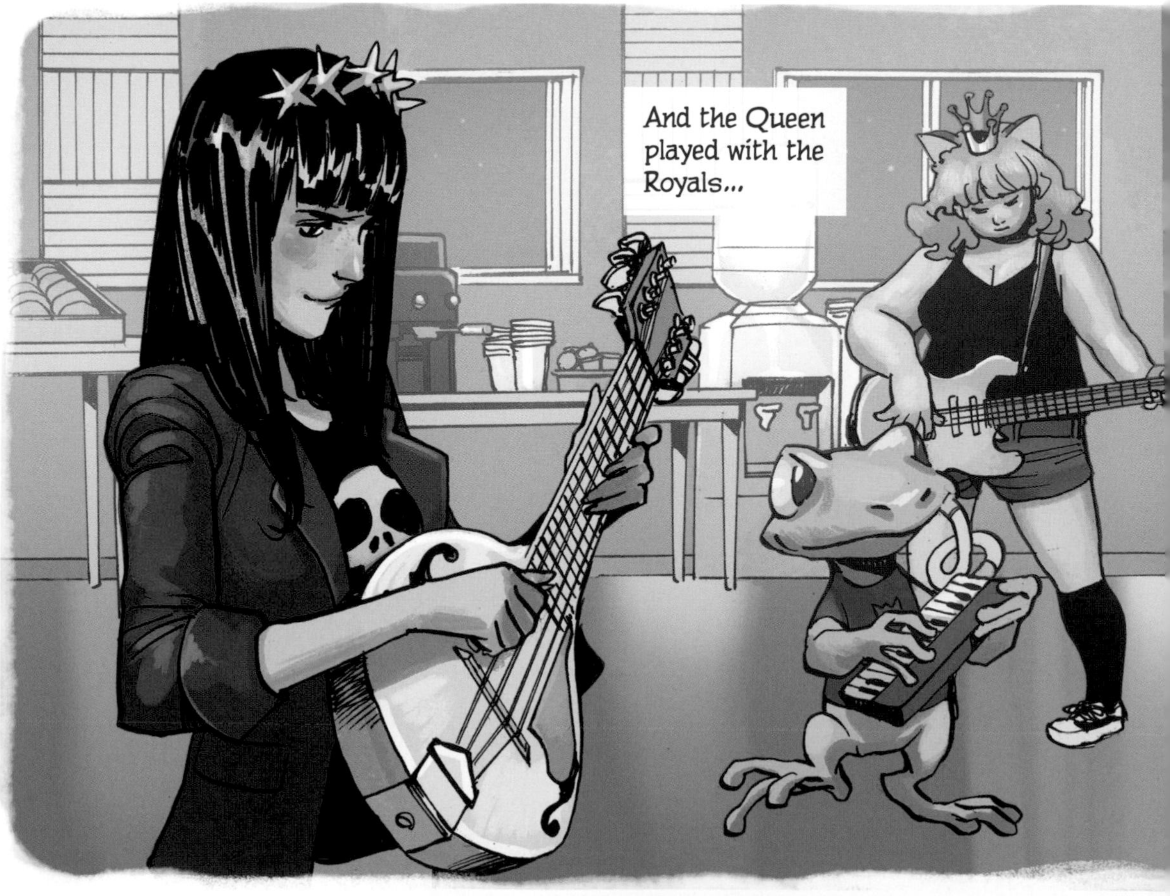
And the Queen played with the Royals...

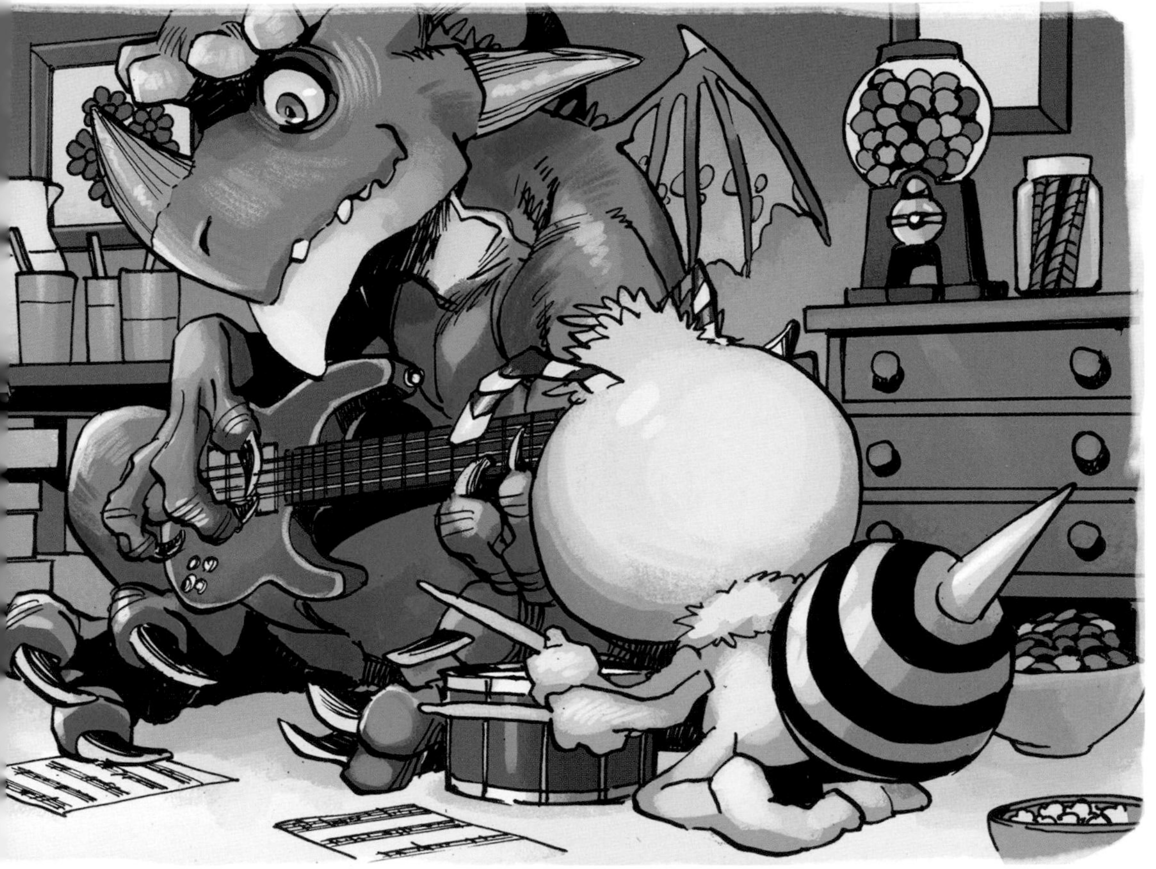

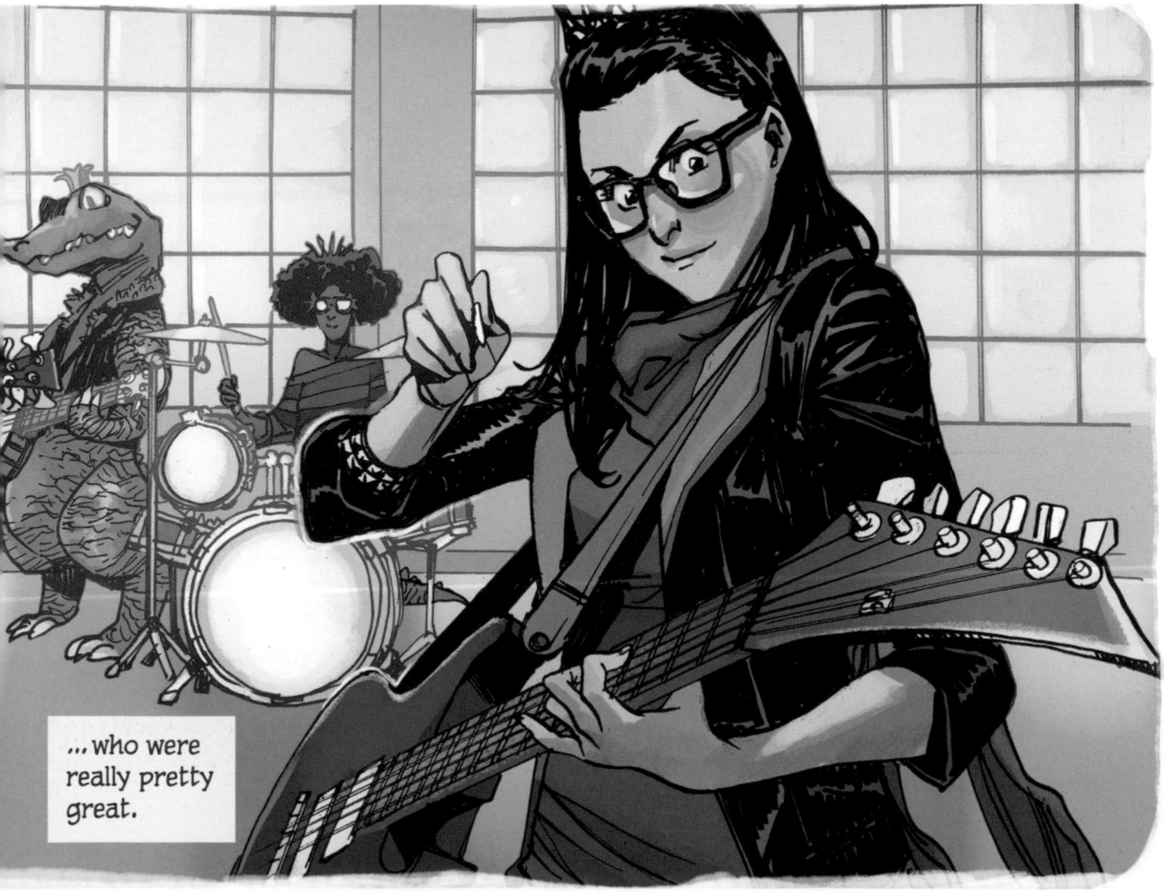
...who were really pretty great.

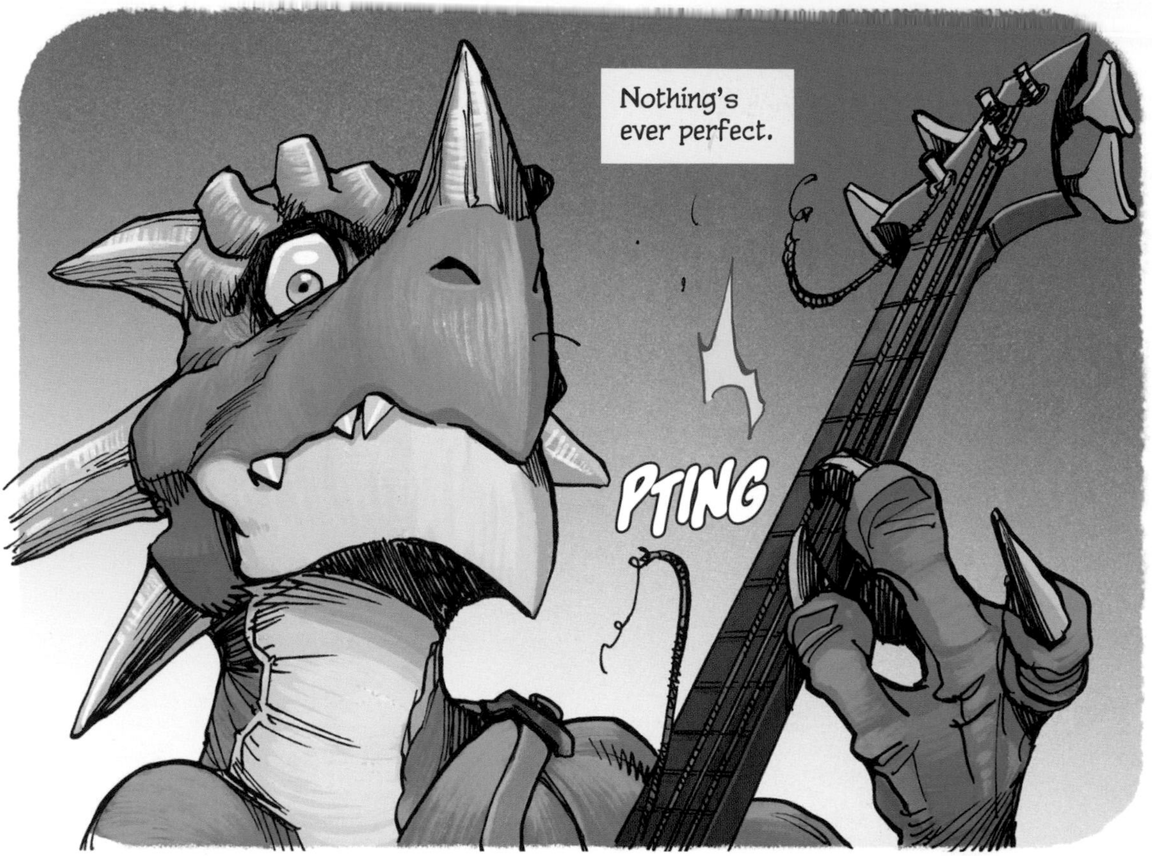
Nothing's ever perfect.
PTING

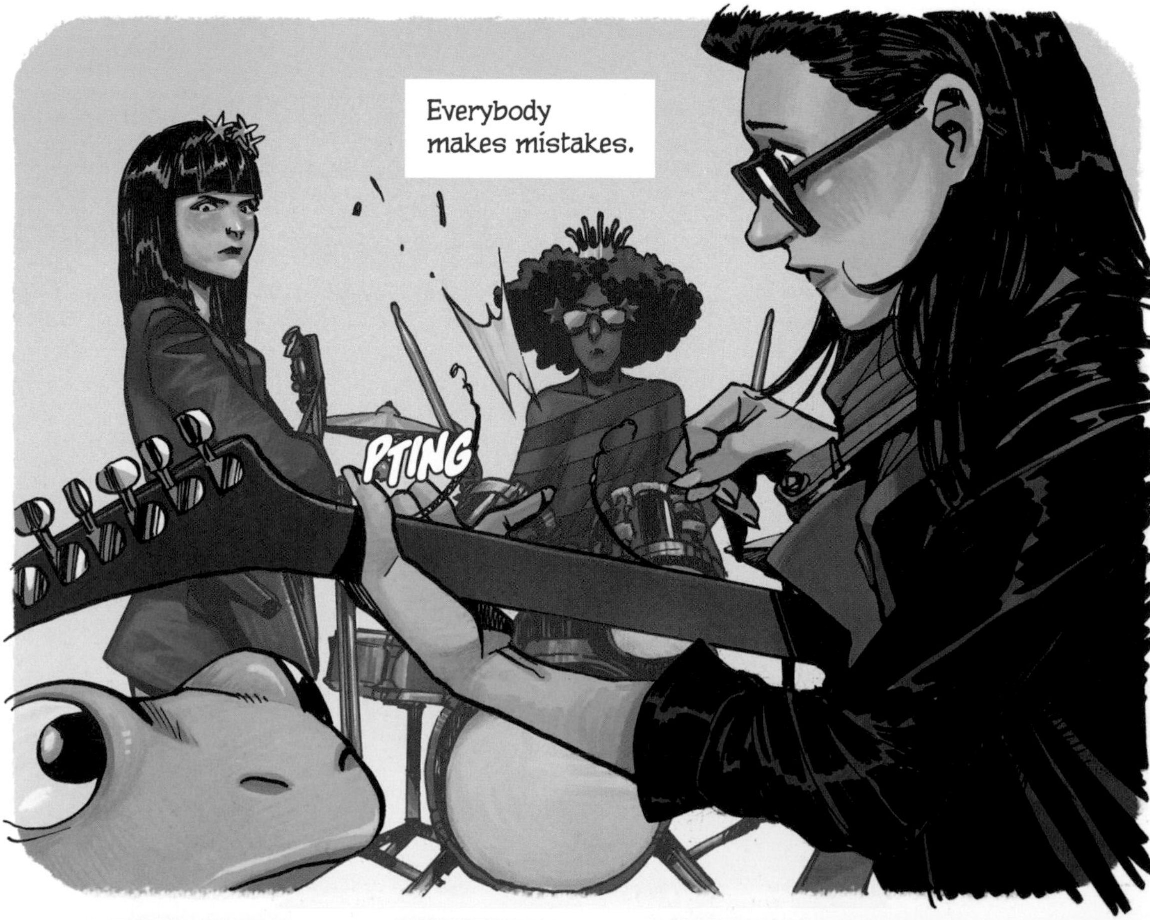
Everybody makes mistakes.
PTING

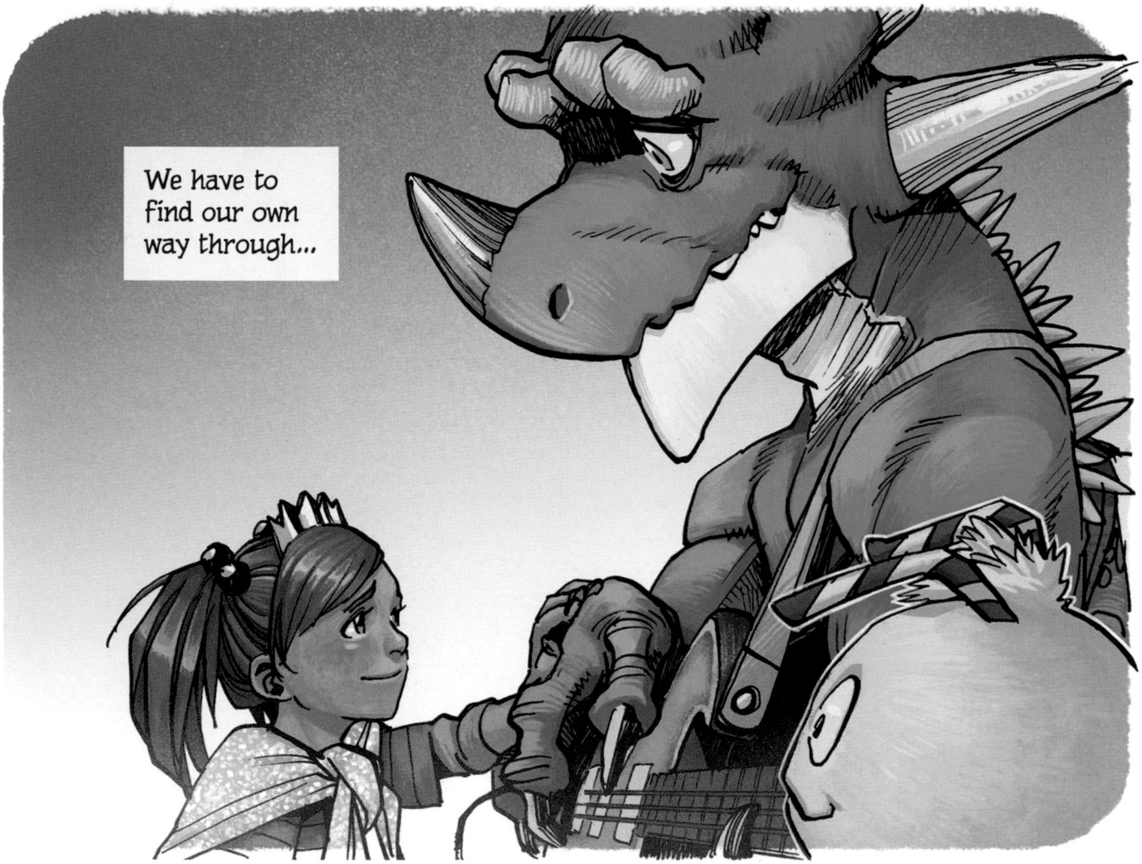
We have to find our own way through...

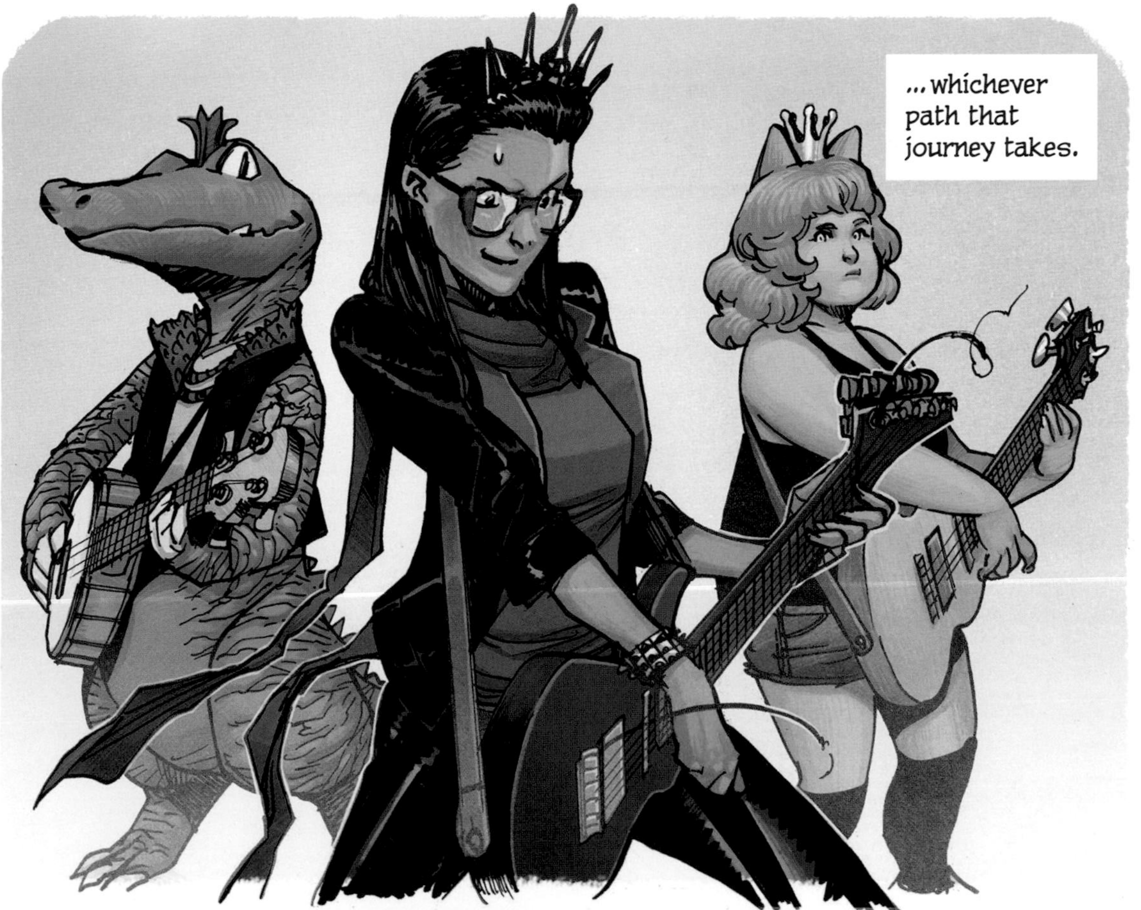
...whichever path that journey takes.

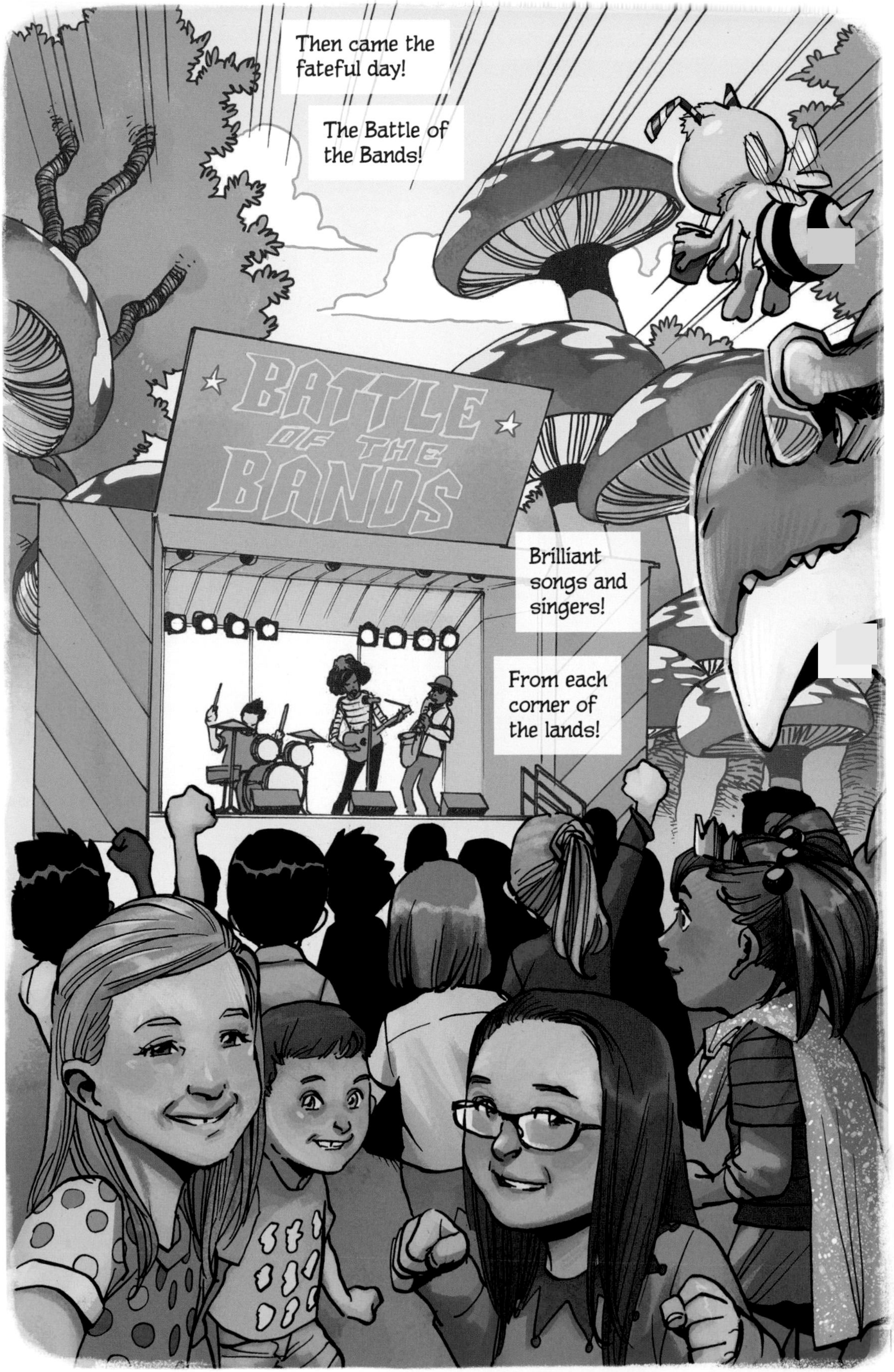
Then came the fateful day!
The Battle of the Bands!
BATTLE OF THE BANDS
Brilliant songs and singers!
From each corner of the lands!

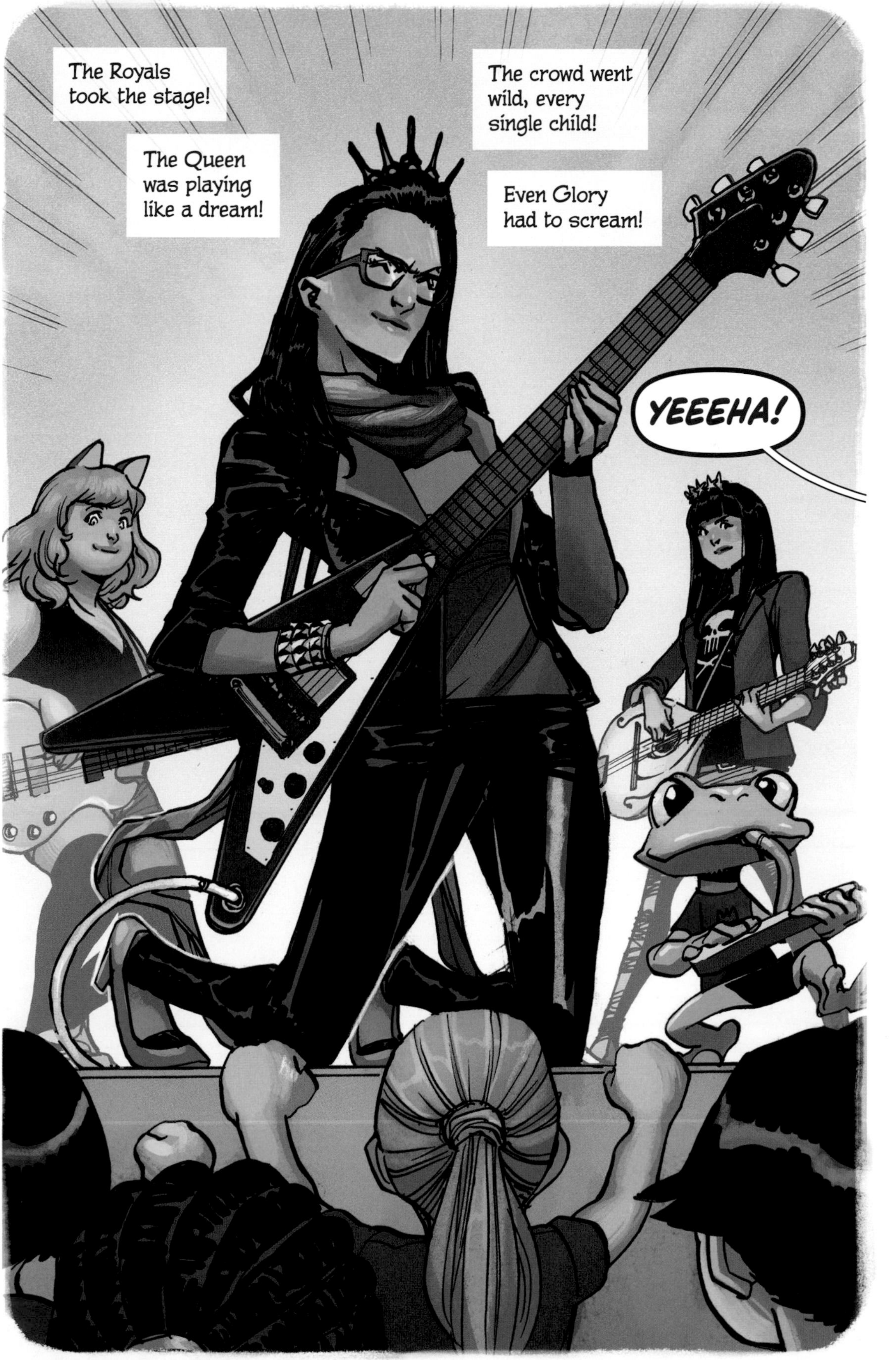
The Royals took the stage!
The Queen was playing like a dream!
The crowd went wild, every single child!
Even Glory had to scream!
YEEEHA!

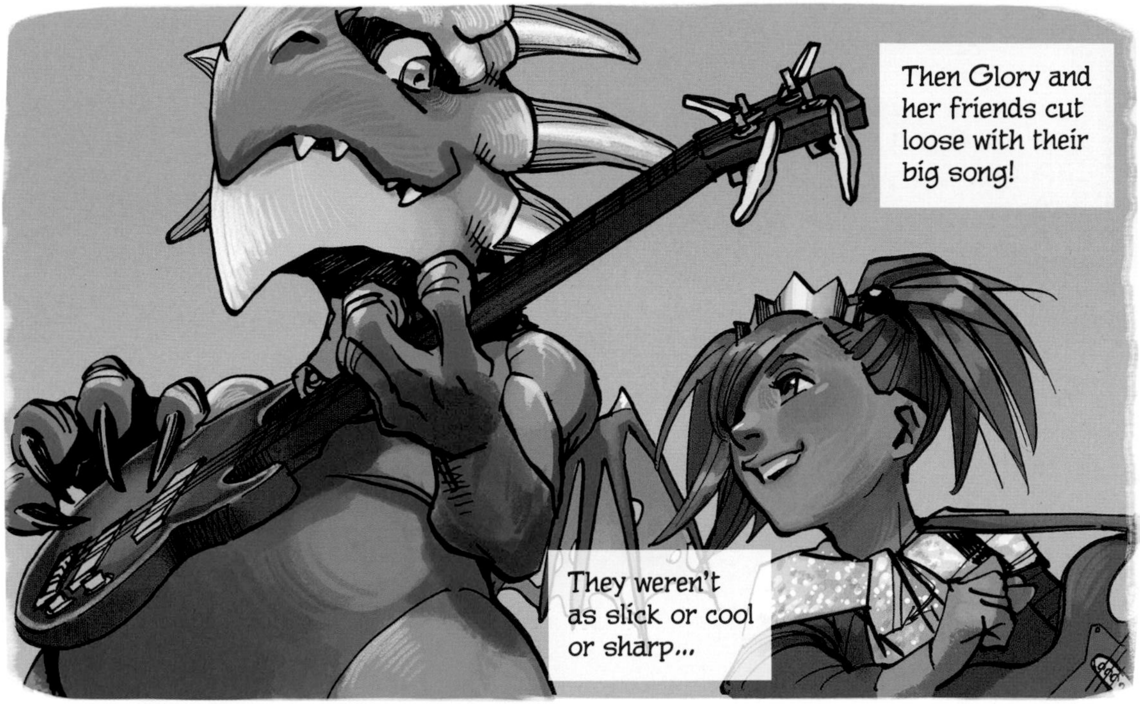
Then Glory and her friends cut loose with their big song!
They weren't as slick or cool or sharp...

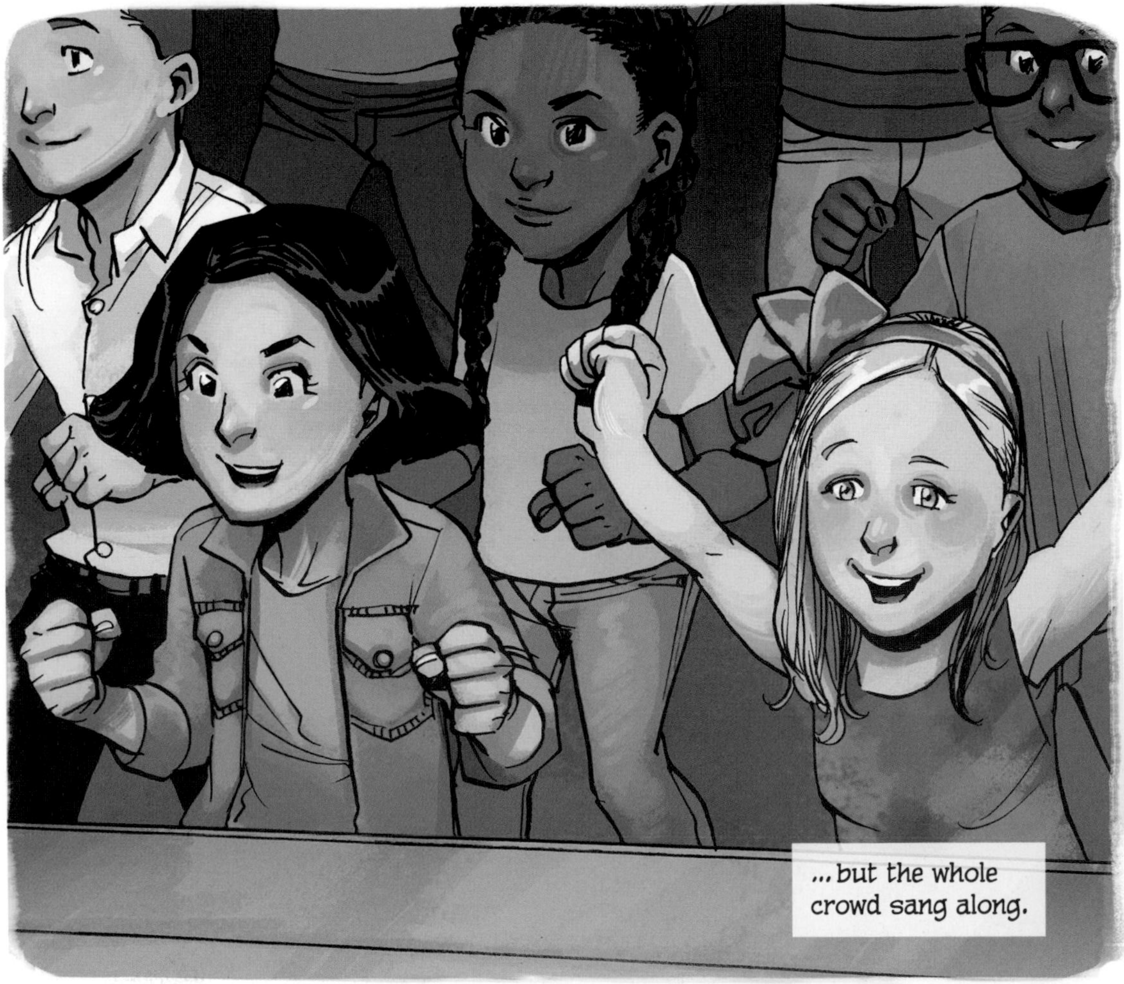
...but the whole crowd sang along.

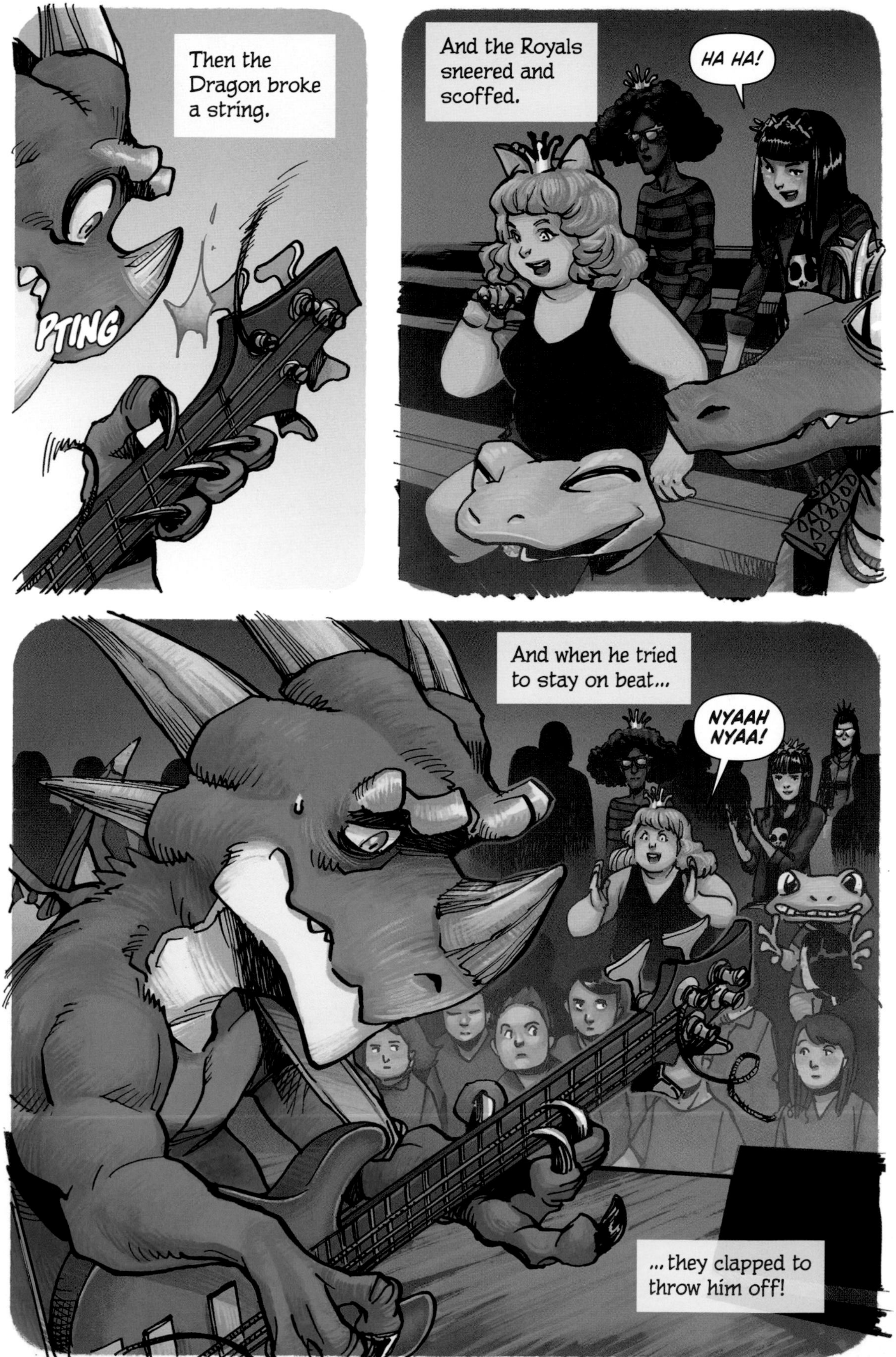
Then the Dragon broke a string.
PTING
And the Royals sneered and scoffed.
HA HA!
And when he tried to stay on beat...
NYAAH NYAA!
...they clapped to throw him off!

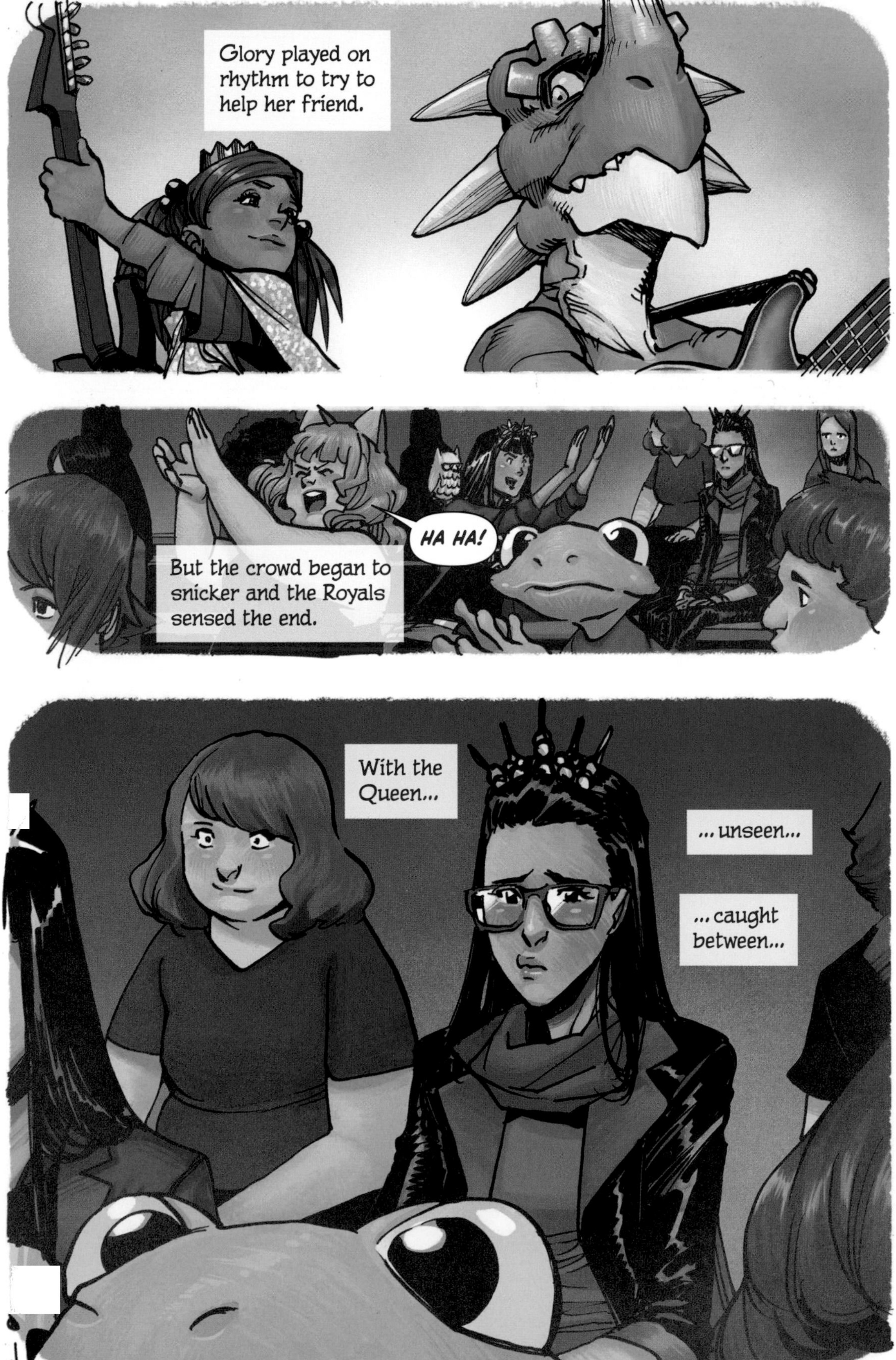
Glory played on rhythm to try to help her friend.
HA HA!
But the crowd began to snicker and the Royals sensed the end.
With the Queen...
... unseen...
... caught between...

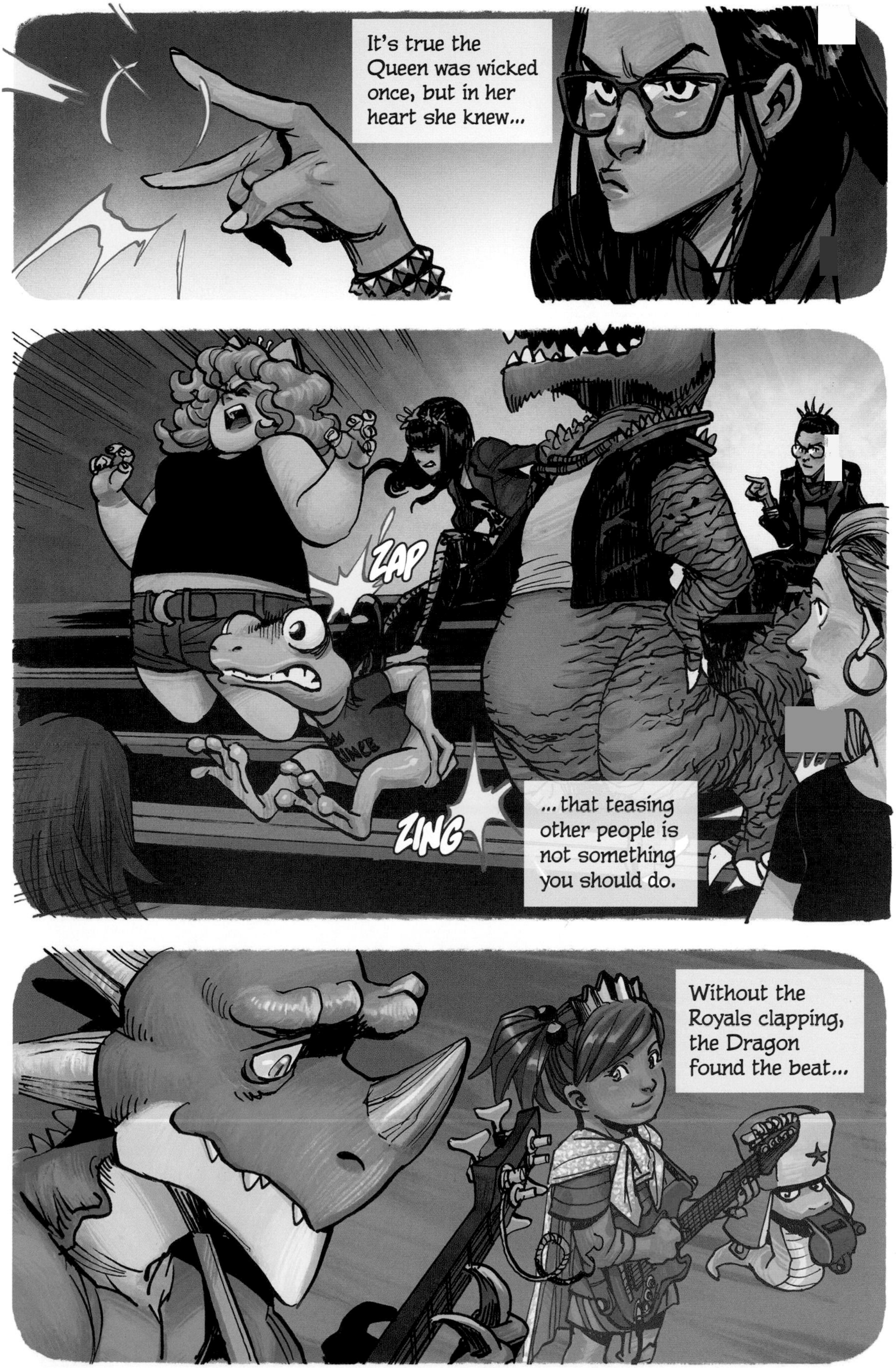
It's true the Queen was wicked once, but in her heart she knew...
ZAP
ZING
...that teasing other people is not something you should do.
Without the Royals clapping, the Dragon found the beat...

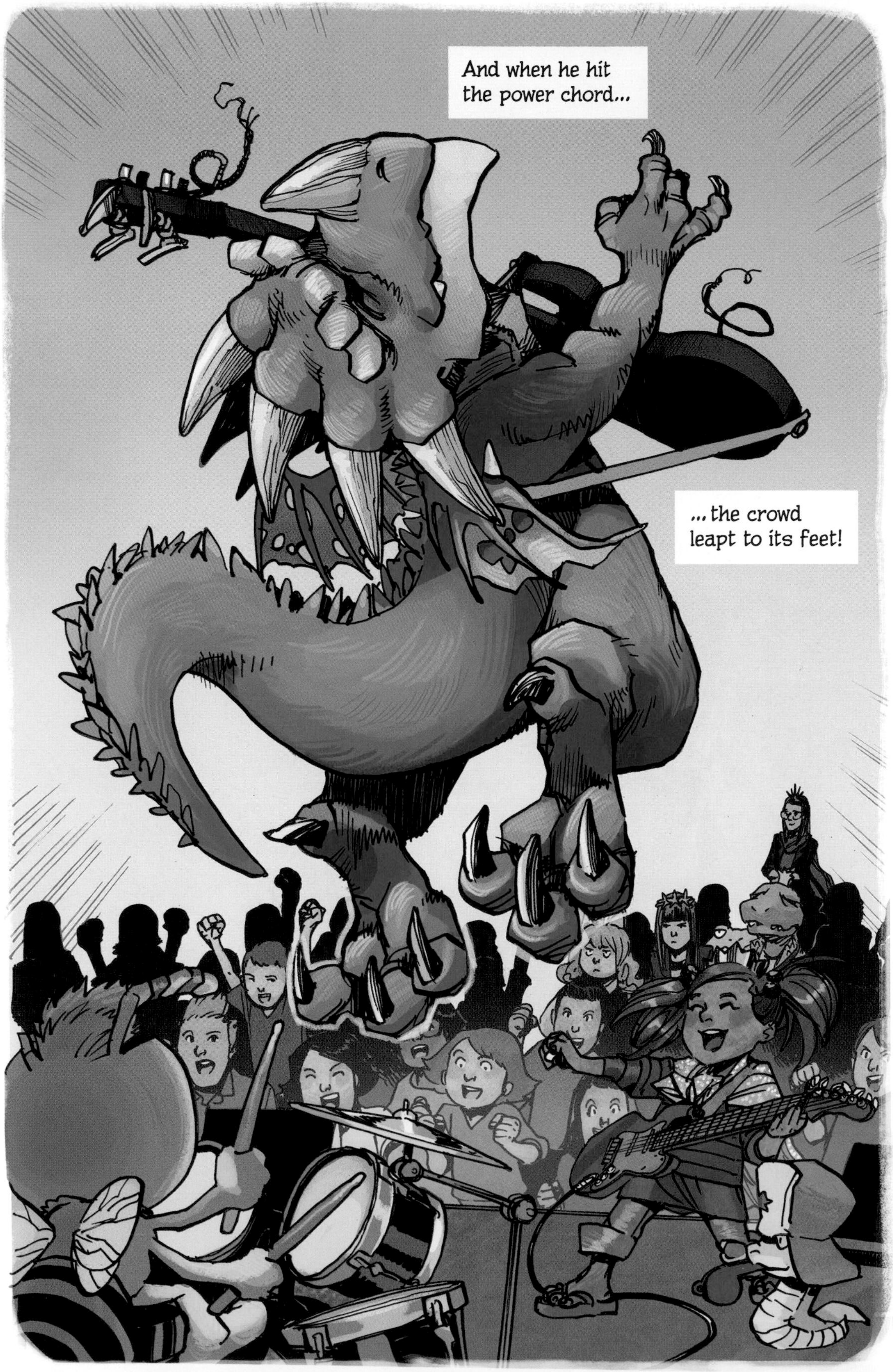
And when he hit the power chord...
...the crowd leapt to its feet!

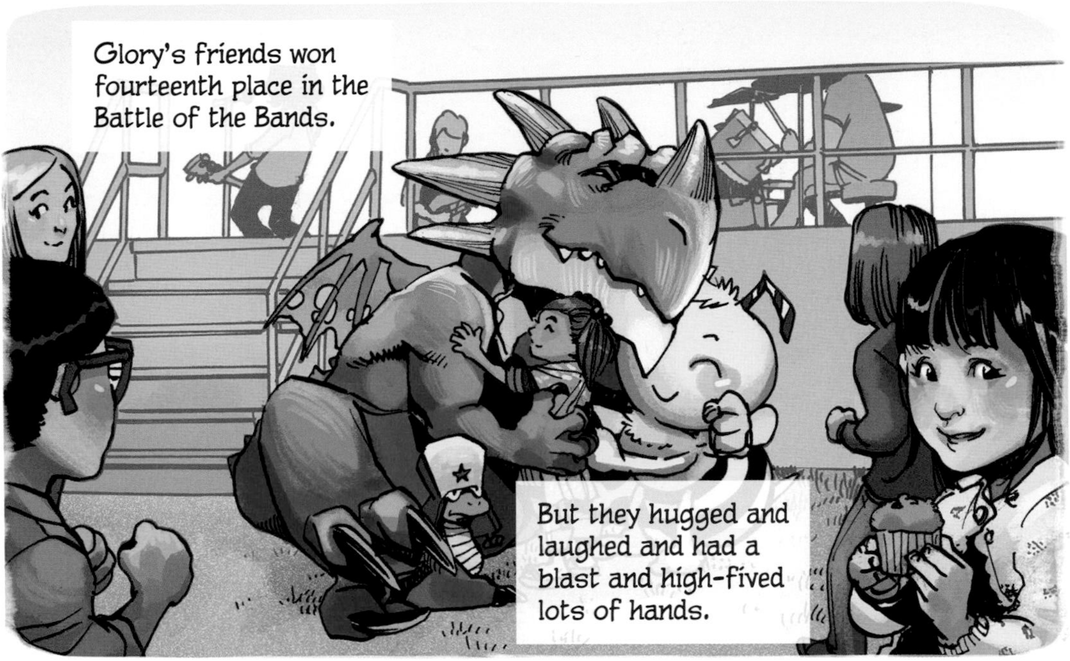
Glory's friends won fourteenth place in the Battle of the Bands.
But they hugged and laughed and had a blast and high-fived lots of hands.

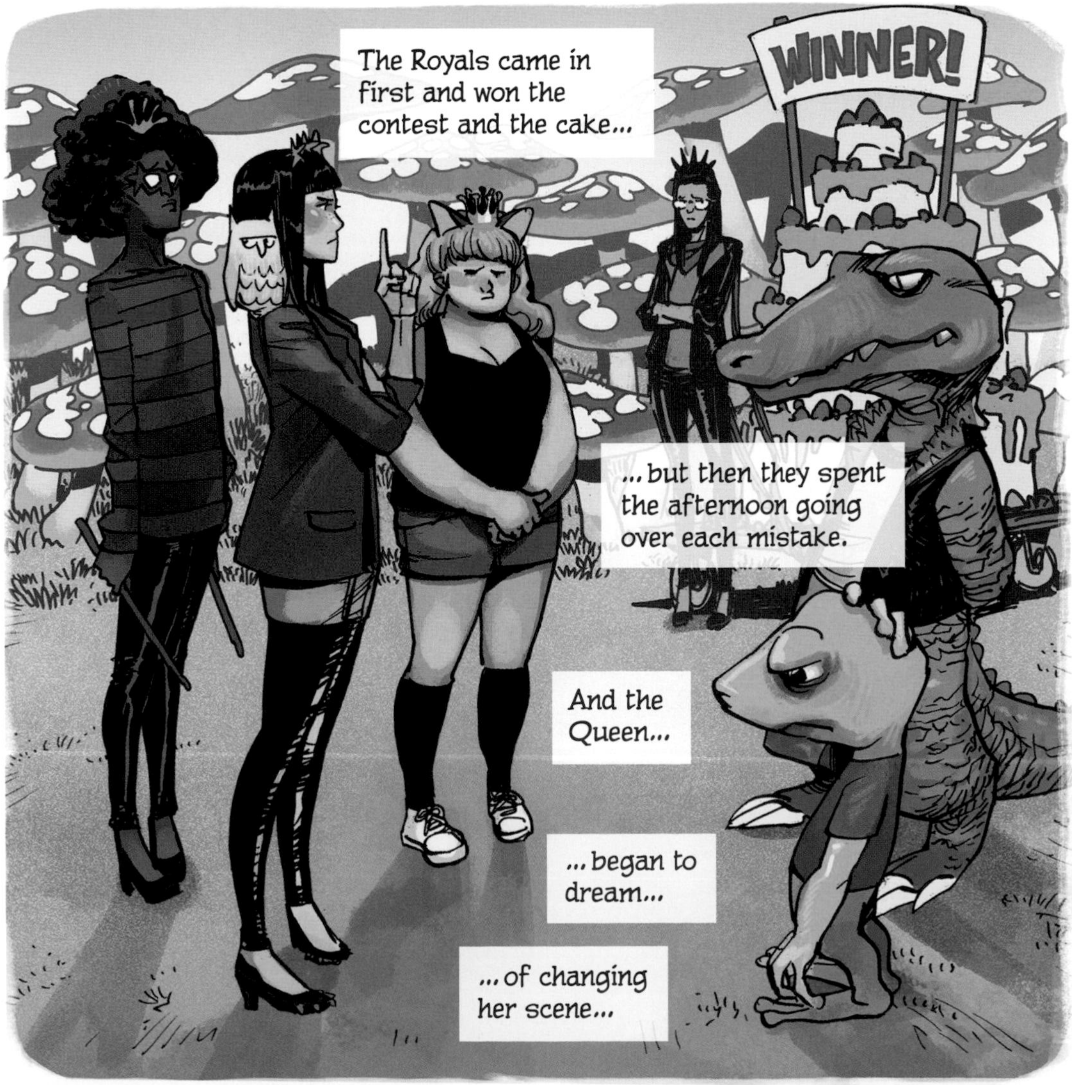
The Royals came in first and won the contest and the cake...
WINNER!
...but then they spent the afternoon going over each mistake.
And the Queen...
...began to dream...
...of changing her scene...

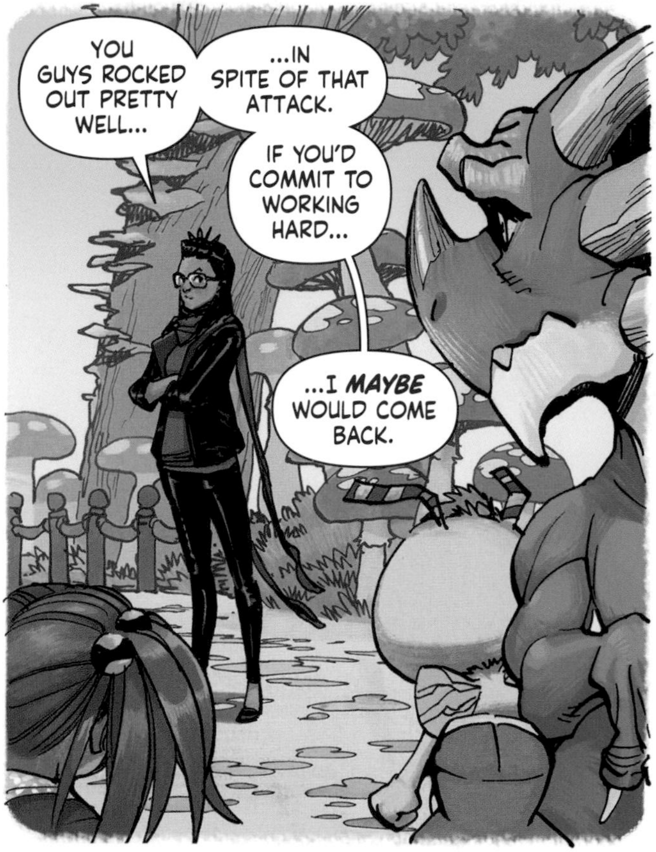
YOU GUYS ROCKED OUT PRETTY WELL...
...IN SPITE OF THAT ATTACK.
IF YOU'D COMMIT TO WORKING HARD...
...I *MAYBE* WOULD COME BACK.

The Dragon beamed with joy and blurted:

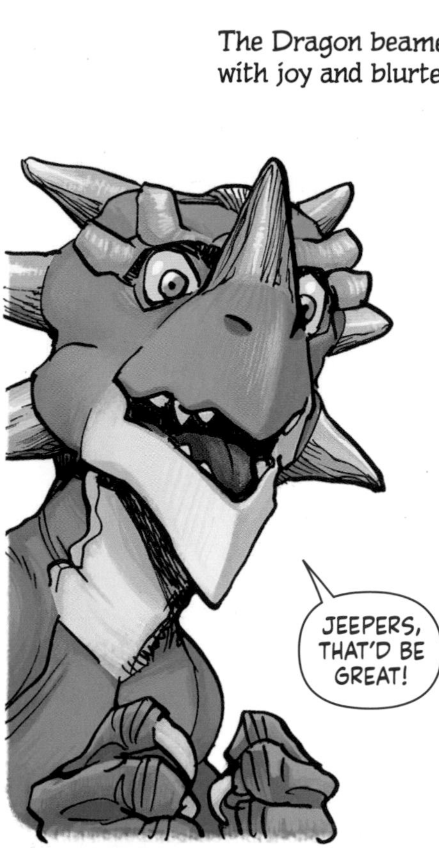
JEEPERS, THAT'D BE GREAT!

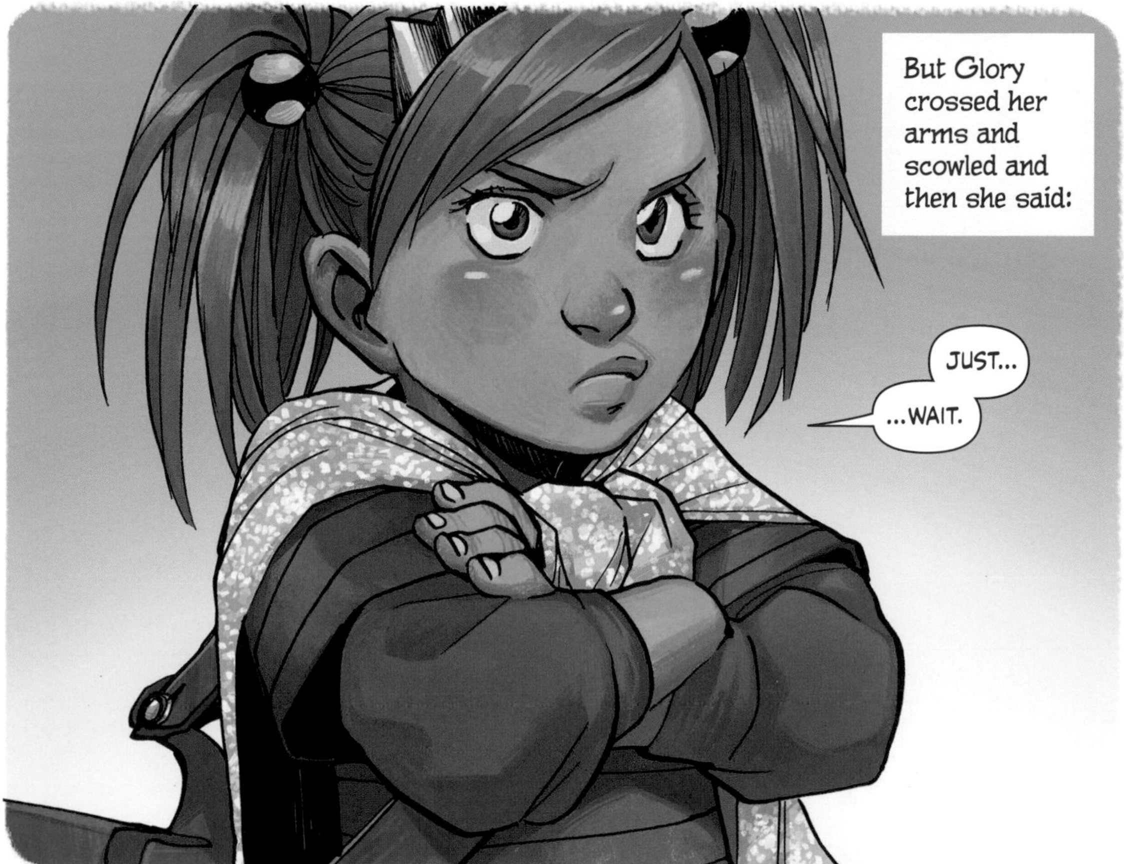
But Glory crossed her arms and scowled and then she said:
JUST...
...WAIT.

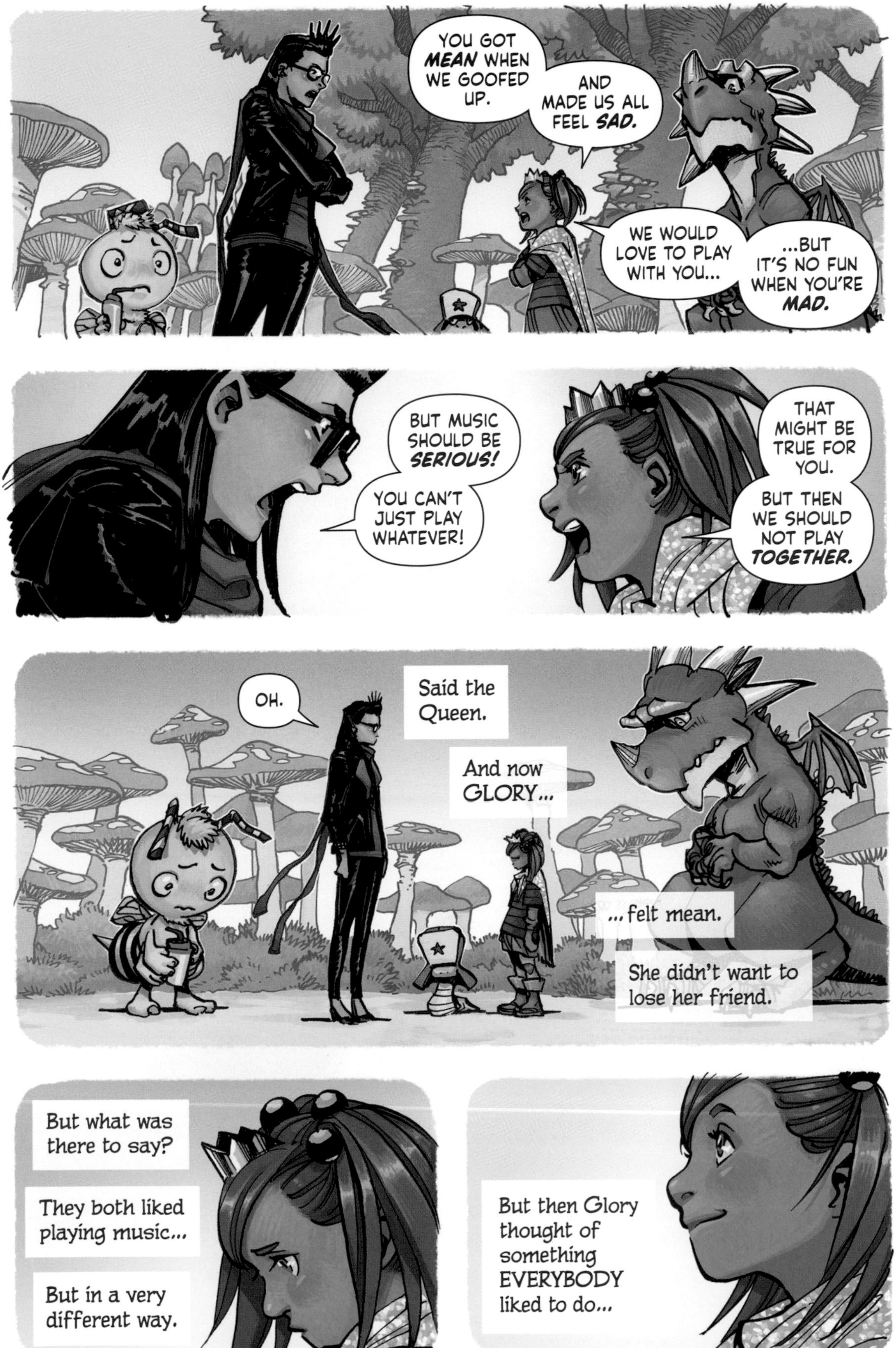
YOU GOT MEAN WHEN WE GOOFED UP.
AND MADE US ALL FEEL SAD.
WE WOULD LOVE TO PLAY WITH YOU...
...BUT IT'S NO FUN WHEN YOU'RE MAD.
BUT MUSIC SHOULD BE SERIOUS!
YOU CAN'T JUST PLAY WHATEVER!
THAT MIGHT BE TRUE FOR YOU.
BUT THEN WE SHOULD NOT PLAY TOGETHER.
OH.
Said the Queen.
And now GLORY...
...felt mean.
She didn't want to lose her friend.
But what was there to say?
They both liked playing music...
But in a very different way.
But then Glory thought of something EVERYBODY liked to do...

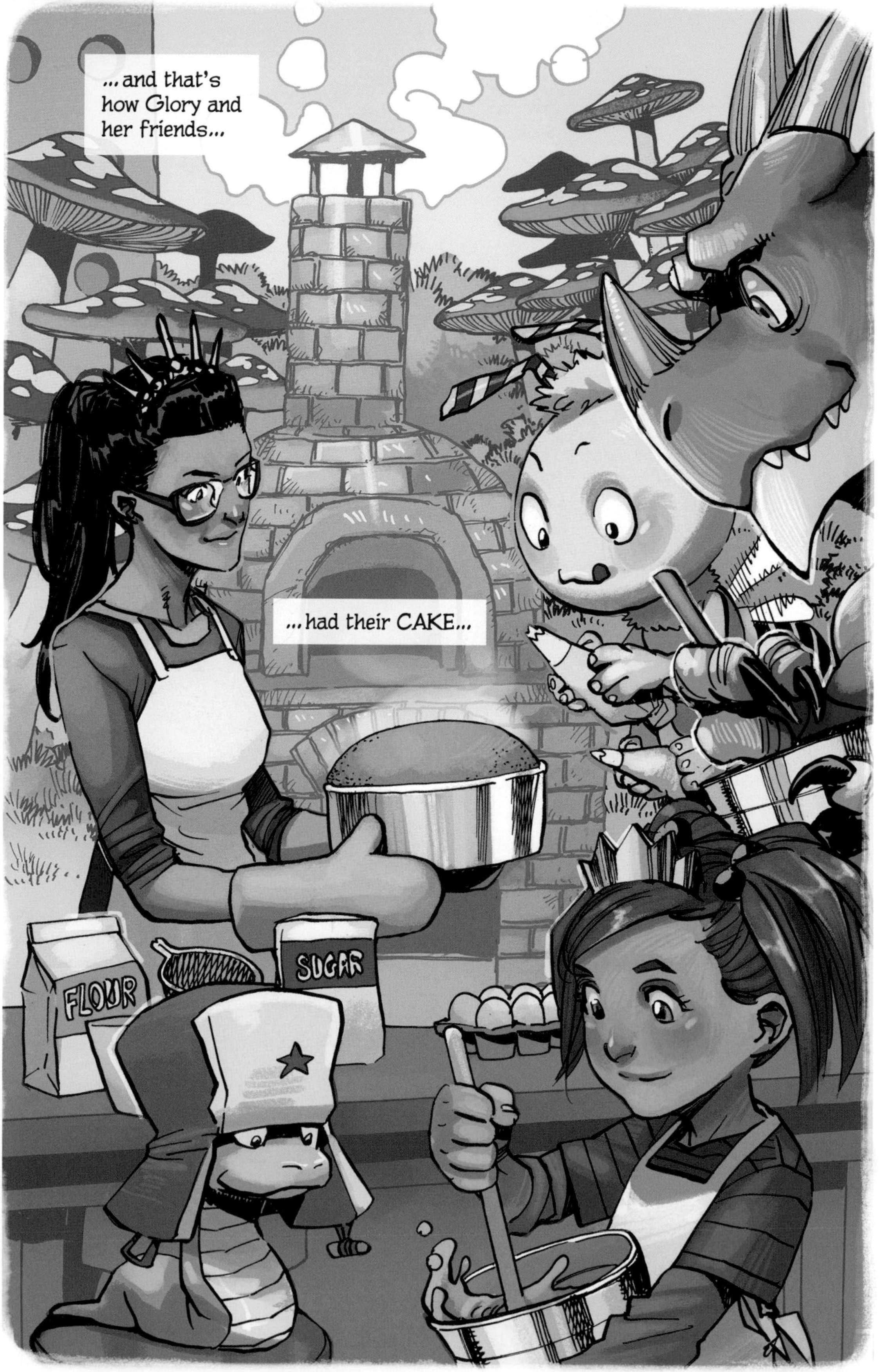
...and that's how Glory and her friends...
...had their CAKE...
FLOUR
SUGAR

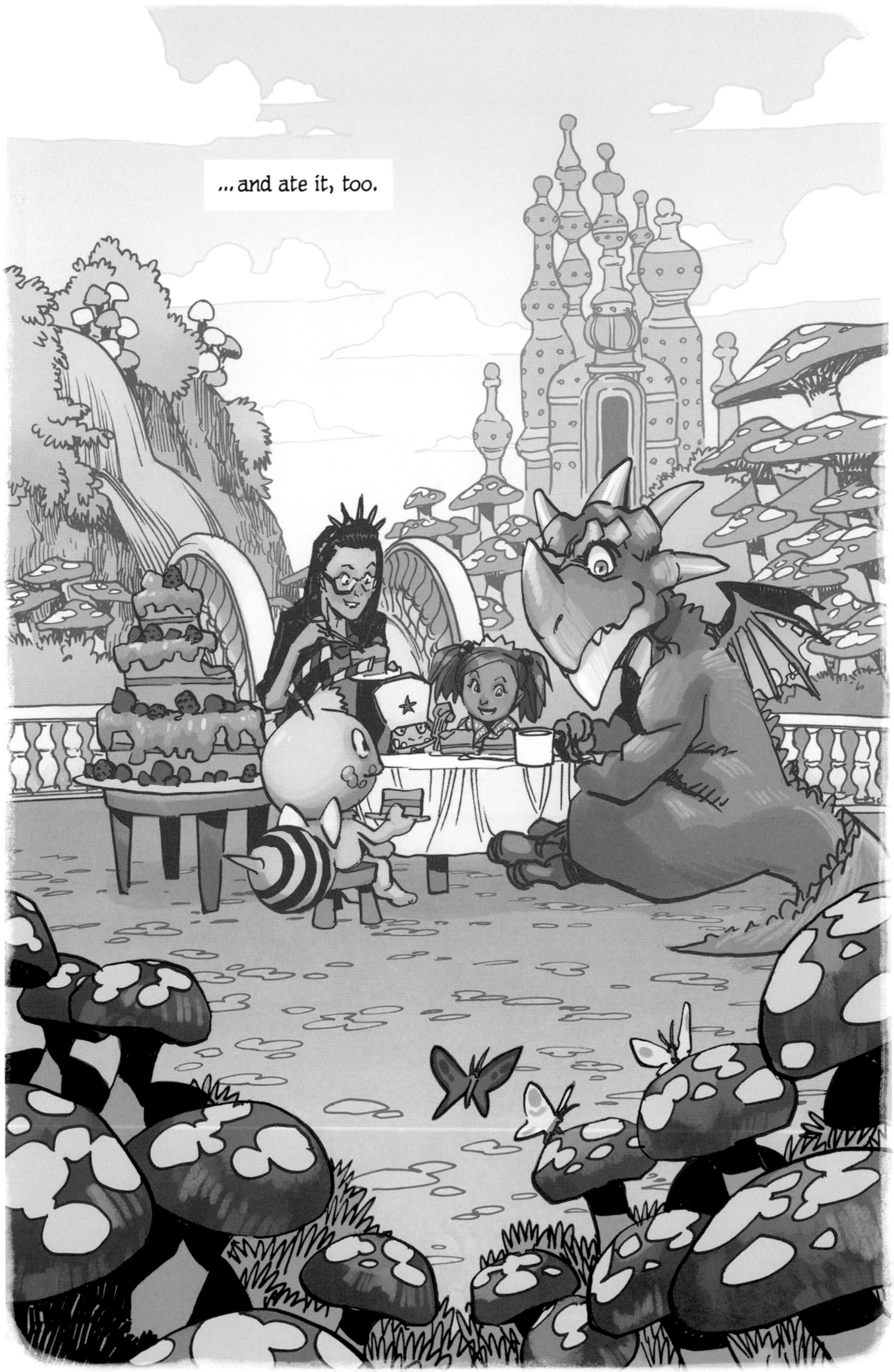
...and ate it, too.

The End.

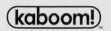

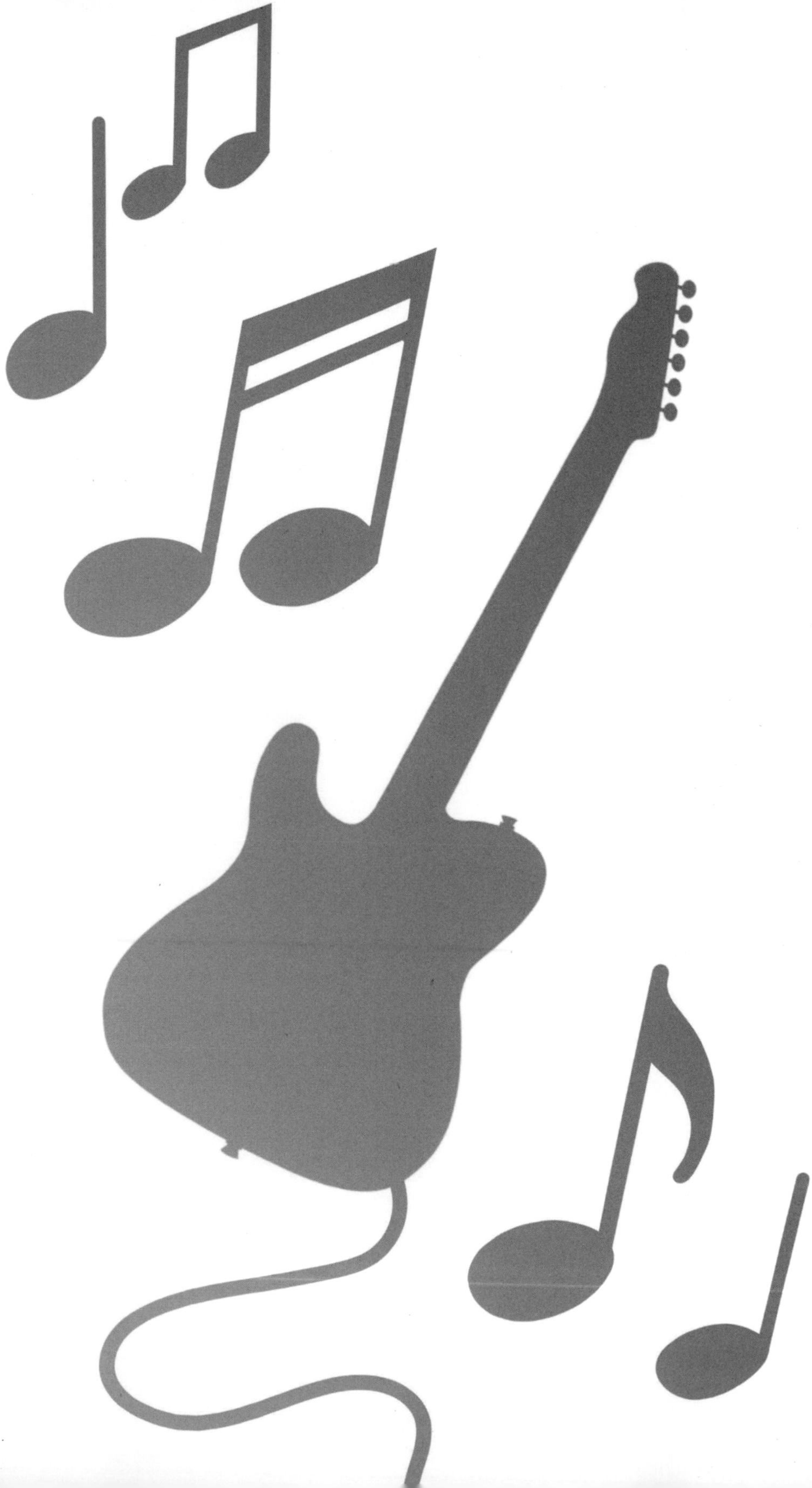

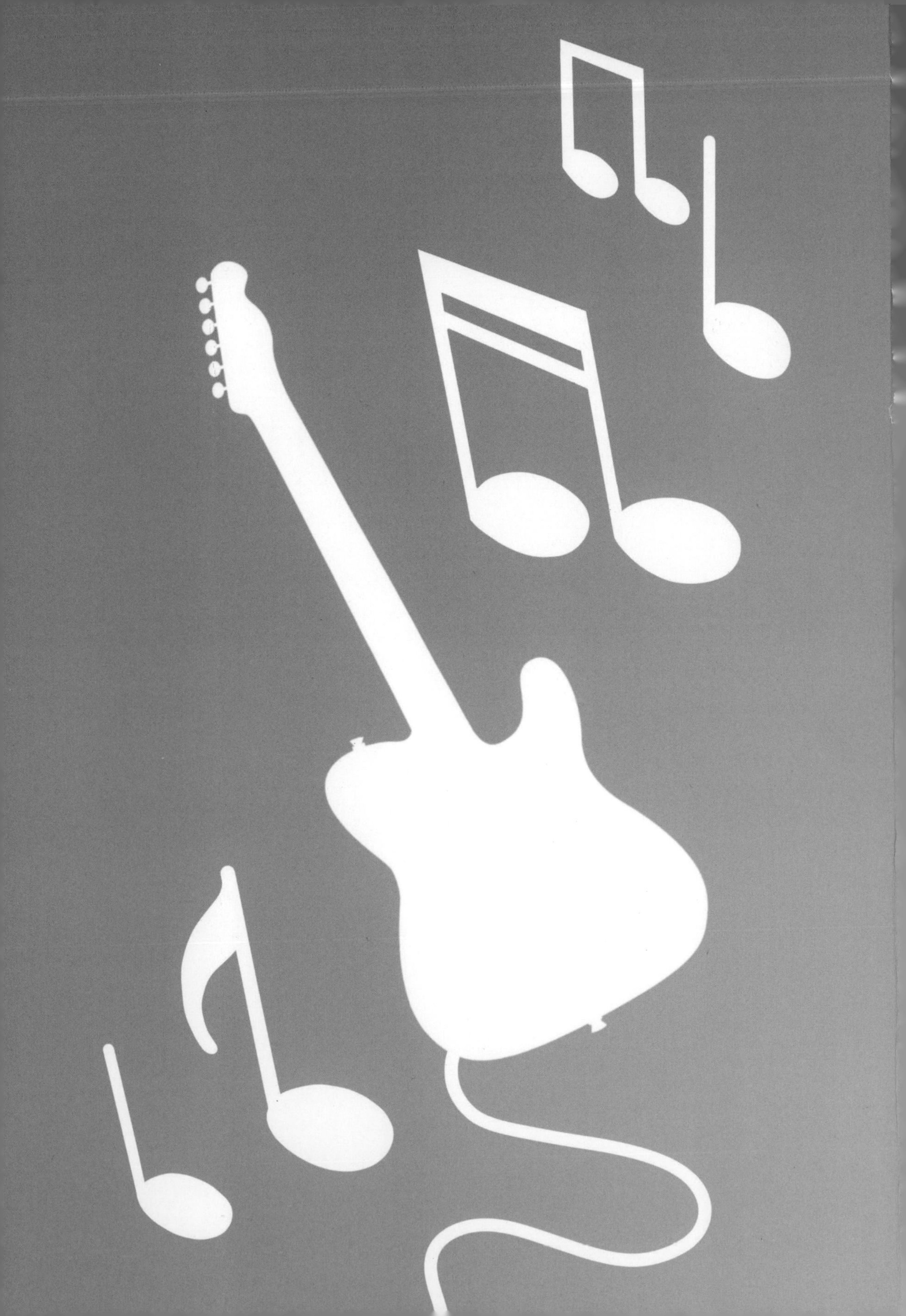